"Let's check out your locker," I said.

We pushed through the swinging doors.

And I thought the smell in the cafeteria was overwhelming.

## NEW CHEMICAL WARFARE!
### Smelly Socks and Wet Towels Studied for Military Use

"It's over here," Angelina said.

She led me between the rows of lockers. I spotted a stray sock here, a notepad there. Some hair scrunchies. A copper bracelet.

Angelina faltered. She looked as if she might faint.

"Angelina, you didn't eat anything at lun

tre

o
th

**GET REAL #7**

# Girl Reporter Gets the Skinny!

### Created by
# LINDA ELLERBEE

AVON BOOKS NEW YORK
*A Division of HarperCollinsPublishers*

A-313

My deepest thanks to Katherine Drew, Anne-Marie
Cunniffe, Lori Seidner, Holly Camilleri, Whitney
Malone, Roz Noonan, Alix Reid, Julia Richardson,
and Susan Katz, without whom this series of books
would not exist. I also want to thank Christopher
Hart, whose book, *Drawing on the Funny Side of
the Brain*, retaught me how to cartoon. At age 11,
I was better at it than I am now. Honest.

*Drawings by Linda Ellerbee*

Avon Books® is a registered trademark
of HarperCollins Publishers Inc.

Library of Congress Cataloging-in-Publication Data
Ellerbee, Linda.
   Girl reporter gets the skinny / created by Linda Ellerbee.
      p.      cm. — (Get real ; #7)
   Summary: School newspaper reporter Casey Smith searches out the
person who is trying to sabotage Trumbull Middle School's star cheerleader, while also puzzling over her friends' constant worrying about
their looks.
      ISBN 0-06-029257-1 (lib. bdg.) — ISBN 0-06-440951-1 (pbk.)
   [1. Cheerleading—Fiction.   2. Beauty, Personal—Fiction.
3. Journalism—Fiction.   4. Schools—Fiction.]   I. Title.
PZ7.E42845 Ghk   2001                                          00-40905
[Fic]—dc21                                                          CIP
                                                                     AC

Typography by Carla Weise
1   2   3   4   5   6   7   8   9   10
❖
First Edition

For the kids,
who always get real

# CHAPTER 1

# Girl Reporter Cheers and Jeers!

MY NAME IS Casey Smith, and I deserved a medal for service way above and beyond. Classes had been over for a full hour already. But had I evacuated the premises? Was I pounding the keys at the *Real News* office, tying up the loose ends of a crackling story? No. I was spending my post-school time doing what?

Coaching a cheerleader.

Yes, you read that right. And yes, this is *that* Casey Smith, ace reporter. Hey—would I lie?

I guess I should explain how I landed in the bizarro world of after-school activities. Especially since I slipped into Ringo's alternate universe voluntarily.

My pal Ringo qualifies as a one-of-a-kind on

many levels. He has an awesomely fractured worldview that hovers just slightly to the left of normal. Just enough distance from run-of-the-mill to provide flashes of brilliance. He's also the only guy cheerleader I know. The only guy cheerleader on the Trumbull Middle School squad.

Actually, he was an alternate, but since he had recently gotten a chance to cheer in a few games, I thought of him as a confirmed Cheerio.

I admit, I tried to discourage him from pursuing his peppy pastime. Okay. I downright hounded him. But did he listen to me? No. See what I mean? He marches to a syncopated beat all his own. Take world, mix it up with hip-hop, add a dose of roots rock, then set the dial to random. That's Ringo.

The rah-rahs were all revved because they were getting ready for some cheerleading competition. I can just imagine the categories: pep, perk, putrid.

Ringo wanted to get extra practice in while they decided what their routine would be. So here I was: Coach Casey.

How could I turn down his request? It appeared taped to my locker in cartoon form:

I am not worthy, but thanks!

Okay. Maybe calling it "coaching" was stretching it. Basically, my job would be to turn the boom box on and off. Ringo's friend Melody would be doing more of the coaching than me.

Because of the unseasonably warm weather, the teams were all meeting outside. I guessed global warming wasn't all bad.

The candy-cane uniforms made the cheerleaders easy to spot. The practice must have just finished. Some of the girls were milling around talking, and others were still doing stunts.

Ringo and Melody were also pretty noticeable off on the sidelines. Melody stood in the bleachers, waving her arms around. I suppose that could be interpreted as coaching, if you use the term really really loosely.

Melody's arm movements made her drapey sleeves flap. Her midnight-blue dress looked kind of medieval. I couldn't figure out how she could turn her head with the wide copper collar around her neck. The effect was kind of Xena meets Shakespeare.

Like Ringo, Melody is her own one-of-a-kind. That's probably what made them gravitate toward each other and why I like her, too. Cookie-cutter kids give me the squeemies.

Maybe there are other sixth graders like Melody back in England, where she's from. But she's a standout here in sleepy little Abbington in the Berkshire mountains of Western Massachusetts.

Next to Ringo and Melody, I must be practically invisible. Brown hair. Brown eyes. Brown freckles. T-shirt (no logo!). Jeans. My Converse high-tops brighten up my monotone existence. Today's pair was a vivid purple. When you're an eleven-year-old in Abbington, you make your statements where you can.

I watched Ringo execute a series of cartwheels as I jogged over. I slid onto the bleacher seat beside Melody's hiking-booted feet. Maybe all her flailing was a reaction to sitting through the entire practice.

"Hi, Casey!" Ringo had finished defying gravity and stood in front of me, grinning. "Thanks for helping."

"No sweat," I replied.

He lifted his arm and sniffed his pit. "Not too much, anyway."

"Eww, Ringo." I winced. "T.M.I. Too Much Information."

Ringo stood with his arms straight up and one knee bent into a deep lunge. He looked ready for take-off.

"Casey?" Melody said. "Tape, please?"

Oops. "Sorry." I reached over and hit Play.

Whew. Tough work.

"Casey," Melody scolded me. "Stay with us."

Even when Melody was bossing me around it sounded so polite I couldn't get annoyed. I wished I could have an English accent. Maybe then whenever my mouth was getting me in trouble, no one would mind so much.

I've been accused of being a little too in-your-face. I prefer to think of myself as someone who tells the truth and nothing but. Not everyone is comfortable with that, but that's what a journalist does. Bites deep to the core of things, then spits it out.

"So, anything interesting happen?" I asked Melody while Ringo went through his paces. "Did one of the rah-rahs dare to lack pep?"

Melody jumped down and sat beside me. "There was a minor flap at the start," she informed me. "There seemed to be a bit of a to-do regarding Angelina's shoes."

I scanned the field for Angelina Carmichael. I knew who she was because for the last few weeks she'd been hobbling around on crutches. She kind of resembled an elf or a fairy—all green eyes and wispy blond tendrils. Melody was right: Angelina was sitting on the sidelines in school clothes.

"Did she practice at all?" I asked.

Melody shook her head.

"Maybe her ankle still hurts," I suggested. Angelina's crutches had only recently disappeared. In fact, Ringo had performed with the squad at the last few games because Angelina was sidelined.

"Do you think Ringo will actually have a chance to take part in the competition?" Melody asked.

I shrugged. "He's only an alternate," I reminded Melody. This was his reason for extra drills. Ringo wanted to come up with something so awesome, they'd just have to put him in.

"I hadn't realized these practices were spectator sports of their own," Melody commented, eyeing people in the stands.

I looked around the stands. "They look mostly like parents." I also recognized a few sixth- and seventh-grade girls who hadn't made the squad. I figured they were boning up so they'd have a better shot next year.

One person I didn't recognize was a pretty African-American girl sitting off to the side. She was fiddling with one of her beaded braids. She looked a little older than we were—maybe she was in eighth grade. She was on the large side, and was one of the most, well, *developed* girls I had seen in middle school.

I was pretty sure she wasn't a student here. I probably would have noticed her before if she was.

Trumbull Middle School isn't exactly a melting pot, as Gary Williams, the sportswriter on *Real News*, has pointed out on a few occasions. He has mentioned how aware he sometimes is of being one of the few black students here.

Speaking of Gary . . . wasn't he supposed to be here? Megan O'Connor, the *Real News* editor in chief, had insisted he cover the cheerleader competition, over his strenuous objections. He was bugged by the "girly" aspect of the meet. For an eleven-year-old boy, he had strong opinions on things manly.

Thinking about Gary led me naturally to thoughts about my own story for the upcoming issue. I didn't have one yet. I picked dirt out from under my nails. Let's see . . . , I thought.

Two of Ringo's fellow Frosted Cheerios, Angelina and Marcy, approached. They stood and studied Ringo's moves.

"That was great!" Angelina said. "You should just try leading with your left foot after you land."

Ringo flipped himself over to us. Whoo. He was making me dizzy.

"Sometimes it's hard to tell my left from my right when I'm upside-down," he told Angelina.

"I know what you mean," Angelina said. "Sometimes when I'm working on complicated moves I draw a little raptor on my right hand."

"A what?" I asked.

"You know," Angelina said, her green eyes all twinkly. "Raptor. It's a kind of dinosaur. I'm better at drawing a stegosaurus, but that wouldn't help me remember which was my right hand."

"Cool. R equals raptor equals right." Ringo nodded.

"Rightski," Angelina chirped.

"Righteous," Ringo responded.

"Right-a-rama," Angelina said, and giggled.

I had to stop this barfsome wordplay before I was totally sick. "Okay, guys."

Melody clapped her hands. "Ringo, we should get back to work. Casey, rewind."

"Rightieo," I said.

Melody raised an eyebrow.

"Sorry. I mean, gotcha." I bent down and worked the tape player.

Ringo seemed more interested in talking than hand-walking. Seemed sensible to me. I'd rather exercise my mental muscles any day. Only I couldn't follow the conversation. He and Angelina were speaking in some secret language involving prehistoric creatures and gymnastic moves.

Don't ask me. I just report the stuff.

Marcy seemed as impatient as Melody to end the Ringo-Angelina chatfest. "Angelina, I have to take off."

"See you later," Angelina said. Marcy trudged back to the locker room minus her friend.

"Next time we'll figure out how to do Jurassic

jumps," Ringo said to Angelina. "Hey, maybe we should work up some doubles moves!"

"Ha!" A voice barked beside me.

I whirled around. Had they added performing seals to the cheerleading squad?

No. This was no cute marine mammal with whiskers. This was a barking mom. Standing next to her was a sullen teenager. Neither looked happy.

"Ha!" the mom barked again.

I wondered if I should toss her a fish.

"Young man," the woman said in a haughty tone. "I can understand why you'd want to pair with Angelina, but believe me, you don't have the skills to partner her."

She must be Angelina's mother. They both had blond hair, only the mom wore it in an old-fashioned preppy high-school style, with bangs and a headband. She had the same big green eyes. But Angelina's overall effect was soft, like an old-fashioned illustration for a fairy tale. Her mom's features were sharp and pointy.

I glanced at Angelina. Yup. The crimson blush covering Angelina's face confirmed it. Only a parent is capable of causing that excruciating level of embarrassment.

I figured that the glowering girl next to Mrs. Carmichael was Angelina's sister. She was also blond, but a stringy, dark blond, with most of her hair in her face. She was a lot heavier than Angelina, and was a seriously sloppy contrast to the neatnik mom. Mrs. Carmichael was crisp enough to be a salad fixin'.

"In fact, Angelina"—Mrs. Carmichael bypassed Ringo and crossed over to her daughter. She wiped an imaginary smudge from Angelina's perfectly clean cheek—"I've been looking into the guidelines for the meet, and we should consider compcting in the solo division as well."

"Mom," Angelina moaned. "I don't want to have to come up with another whole routine. I'll be lucky if I catch up in time as it is."

"Nonsense," Mrs. Carmichael said. "You can do anything you set your mind to."

"Can we go?" Angelina's sister demanded.

Mrs. Carmichael ignored the request. Her brow furrowed as she studied Angelina. "How did you change so quickly?" she asked, tugging with a frosted fingernail at the sleeve of Angelina's shimmery oversized blouse.

"Uh . . . I . . . " Angelina twisted her wrists around in her cuffs.

Mrs. Carmichael crossed her arms over her chest. "You *did* practice, didn't you? Coach Seltzer allowed you to participate, didn't she?

You gave her the doctor's permission slip?"

"I . . . I couldn't find my sneakers," Angelina blurted.

"What?" Mrs. Carmichael didn't bark this time. She screeched. She screeched so loudly that heads swiveled in our direction. If it was possible to turn any redder, Angelina did.

Lucky for her, there weren't too many people still left on the field. The stands were basically empty now.

"Oh, what a crisis," her sister said sarcastically.

"Lauren," Mrs. Carmichael snapped. Then she turned back to Angelina. "What do you mean, you couldn't find your sneakers? I know you brought them to school."

"I . . . I . . . I don't know," Angelina muttered.

"Are you saying you lost them? Or did someone steal them?"

"They were in my locker and then they weren't anymore," Angelina said.

"Well, I'm going to talk to your coach about this! We can't have thieves stealing your things!"

Mrs. Carmichael stomped off to speak with the coach, dragging Angelina with her. Lauren flopped down on the bleachers nearby and put on some headphones.

"Poor Angelina," Ringo murmured.

"I wonder what happened to her shoes?" Melody said.

Ringo plopped down beside us on the bench. He glanced around to be sure no one would hear him. "I know what happened to them," he whispered.

"Did they take a field trip back to the land of the dinosaurs?" I asked. Okay, I wasn't interested in Angelina's missing sneakers. They did not register on the *Real News* Richter scale.

"I have the sneakers," Ringo confessed. "They're in my locker."

# Sneakers Leave Trail into Boys' Locker Room!

MY EYEBALLS BOINGED out of my head. Really. If they hadn't been attached, they would have landed in Ringo's lap.

Melody sputtered. Funny, an English accent doesn't do a lot to improve spit.

"Why would you steal Angelina's sneakers?" I demanded.

Ringo's face squished up like he'd swallowed a bug. "I didn't steal them," he declared. "She gave them to me. She wanted to hide them."

Now I was really confused. "Why would she want to do that?"

"Actually, we were keeping them as evidence for you!" he said.

Okay. Now I was interested. "What do you mean, evidence?"

14

"Angelina told me that when she put on her sneakers, she found out somebody had smashed eggs in them," Ringo explained. "Raw eggs. Sticky, gooey, smelly—"

"We get the picture," I said. "So why the secrecy?"

He glanced over at Lauren, but she seemed miles away. Her head bobbed to tunes on her Walkman.

"Her mom." Ringo shrugged. "Angelina's got another pair at home. But you saw how her mother gets. Angelina doesn't like to set her off."

"That I understand. But still, if someone egged my shoes, I'd be after them big time." I'd make such a loud noise I'd drown out even Mrs. Carmichael.

"Shh," Ringo shushed me. "Don't spread this around, okay?"

I was hurt. "I can keep a secret. Just because I'm a reporter with a responsibility to report doesn't mean I can't keep my mouth shut."

"Shh!"

Then I saw why Ringo was re-shushing me. Gary Williams was jogging toward us.

"Hey, Casey, moving in on my beat?" he asked me.

I squinted up at him. He stood in the exact spot where looking at him put the sun in my eyes. I hate that.

"Dream on, dude," I told him. "The story is all yours. Only you'll do a better job if you actually manage to get to practice. You missed it today."

"I had a game," he protested.

"I hate to keep having to point this out to you, Gary," I retorted. "The teams all do just fine when you're not there. It's not that critical to warm the bench. Although maybe it will be now that the weather is turning cooler."

"Can it, Smith."

A gaggle of cheerleaders wandered over to us. When it was just Melody, Ringo and me, no one noticed us. As soon as Gary appeared, instant squad.

I could think of two explanations for the squad roundup. One: the cute factor. A lot of girls think Gary is cute. He might be, if he could ever stop broadcasting total ego. The other reason? Media seekers. They knew Gary covered sports for *Real News*. I figured a few of them were angling for extra coverage. After all, isn't the whole point of cheerleading to have people pay attention to you? Wouldn't they pay even more if you were in the school newspaper?

Marcy reappeared in her regular clothes. She made a beeline toward Gary. She twirled her long red hair between her fingers and smiled at him like he hung the moon.

Ugh.

Luckily, Gary had to get home. His exit scattered the rah-rahs to the winds.

"Now, Ringo, let's try it again from the top," Melody suggested. I never realized what a one-track mind she could have.

I dutifully hit Rewind. "I can't stay much longer," I warned. I couldn't take much more.

I glanced over to where Mrs. Carmichael was blasting Coach Seltzer. The coach was handling it pretty well, only that seemed to aggravate Mrs. Carmichael. Have you noticed that if you stay calm while someone yells at you, the other person goes even more crazy?

Angelina said something to her mom and hurried back over to us.

"Casey, I'm glad you're still here." She glanced over at Melody. "Uh, would it be okay if we talked in private?"

Melody looked surprised, then frowned.

"Melody's cool," Ringo assured her.

I was glad to see him vouch for his friend.

"Oh. Okay." She gave Melody a little smile. "If Ringo says you're operating on the same plane, I'll orbit with you."

Melody did not smile back. Me, I just tried to translate. I had a feeling I understood what Ringo saw in her. They spoke the same ring-a-ding lingo.

"Ringo thought . . . uhm, well, we have a story for you to investigate."

I smirked. "What's that? The link between missing brain cells and cheerleading?"

Melody snickered, then covered her mouth with her hand.

Angelina took a step backward as if I had smacked her. She flushed pink.

"Cold, Casey," Ringo admonished me. I suddenly felt bad. Which shocked me. I made cracks like that all the time.

Wow. Angelina had some *niceness* power over people. She made you want to be nice to her. A lot like Ringo.

"It was just a joke," I protested. "So what's this story? Is it about your missing sneakers? Ringo already filled us in that he's the one who made them disappear."

"Yeah." She gave him a "my hero" kind of smile.

"That doesn't sound like a story for the newspaper to me," Melody muttered.

I agreed with her. "So there's no mystery here. Nothing to investigate."

"Sure there is," Ringo said. "Who did it, for starters."

"Some prankster," I said.

Angelina sank down to the bleacher and gazed at her hands. "Egging my sneakers isn't the only thing that's happened," she confessed.

"It's like inanimate objects have it in for her," Ringo said. "Almost like a voodoo curse."

"Ringo, I write for *Real News*, not *The X-Files*."

"Things have happened that I just can't explain," Angelina said.

"You see?" Ringo cut in. "Unexplained phenomena."

"Like what?" I demanded.

"First, there was my sprained ankle," Angelina said.

"Isn't that simply one of the hazards of cheerleading?" Melody asked. She sounded irritated.

Angelina shrugged. "I tripped over a pipe. It wasn't there when I went onto the field."

"Then her cheer book went AWOL," Ringo said. "And then her sneakers got egged." He shuddered. "It's as if the cosmos is telling her not to cheer. Which doesn't make any sense, since she's so good."

"Thanks," Angelina said. "But I'm thinking maybe I should listen to the message."

It did sound like something was going on all right. Only it sounded like typical middle school stunts.

"I don't know," I said. "Gary talks about this kind of goofing around among team members all the time."

"There is another theory," Ringo said. His eyes flicked to Angelina, then back to me. "Someone is out to get Angelina."

# Cheerleader Target of Cruel Attacks!

RINGO AND ANGELINA now had my full attention.

"Please help me, Casey," Angelina said. "I'd hate to have to quit. Cheerleading is really important to me."

"What can *I* do?" I asked.

"You're so good at getting to the bottom of things," Angelina said. "Ringo thought that if you figure out who's doing this, I can get them to back off."

"Why hasn't your coach done anything?" Melody asked.

"I . . . I haven't told her." Angelina plucked at her leggings. "I thought if I ignored the problem, the person would stop."

Melody nodded. "Sometimes that's the best way to deal with a practical joker. Ignore them and they'll go away. Toodle-oo."

"But it hasn't worked," Ringo said. "And with the competition coming up, Angelina needs to totally focus on her own stunts, not on someone else's."

The competition. That made that familiar little tingle at the tip of my nose begin twitching. The one that told me I was edging up to a story.

"When did all this start?" I asked Angelina. I had a hunch I already knew the answer to that.

Her mouth pursed as she thought back. "A few weeks ago."

"When did the squad find out they were going to compete?" I pressed.

Light dawned. "Around the same time."

"I think we've just nailed the motive," I declared.

Mrs. Carmichael stalked over to us. I stole a glance at Coach Seltzer. The coach looked rattled but was still standing. Angelina's sister, Lauren, pulled the headphones from her ears.

"All right, Angelina," Mrs. Carmichael ordered. "I will coach you myself for the next hour. You need to get back into shape after your injury."

"But . . ." Angelina looked surprised.

"Mom," Lauren whined. "You said we were

just going to pick up Angelina and go straight home."

"Our plans have changed," Mrs. Carmichael snapped. She narrowed her eyes as she studied Angelina. "Lauren," she barked, "give Angelina your sneakers. Angelina, those leggings will be fine to work out in."

"You want my *shoes*?" Lauren asked in astonishment.

Mrs. Carmichael held out her hand to Lauren and snapped her fingers. Lauren gaped at her.

This was intense. I'd never witnessed such a full-blown conflict of wills. Lauren looked ready and able to fight.

But Mrs. Carmichael was a formidable foe. I could practically hear a low growl in the back of her throat. The words "pit bull" came to mind.

Lauren caved. "I've got an extra kidney I'm probably not using," she muttered. She yanked off her sneakers and handed them over to her mom.

"They're a little big, but they should do." Mrs. Carmichael handed Angelina the sneakers.

I noticed Angelina didn't look at Lauren at all while she changed into the sneakers.

"You know, I have a life, too," Lauren shouted at Mrs. Carmichael.

"Watching television? Stuffing yourself at the

mall?" Mrs. Carmichael said. "I'm sorry, Lauren, but what Angelina is doing is important."

"Important? Jumping around in a little skirt? That's what you consider important?"

Lauren had my total sympathy. But I really didn't feel like watching a total family feud.

"I gotta go," I said to Melody and Ringo. I picked up my backpack. "Coming?"

Melody grabbed the boom box and looked expectantly at Ringo.

"Nah," he said. "I think I'll stick around and help Angelina practice. Sometimes we do things that require partners."

"That's very nice of you," Mrs. Carmichael said. "But we wouldn't want Angelina to pick up bad habits."

"Oh, I quit chewing on pencils last year," Ringo assured her.

I fumed. Mrs. Carmichael acted as if Ringo was going to give her precious Angelina cooties. All he was trying to do was help out a friend.

"Yes, Ringo," I said. "That's an excellent idea. Angelina always performs better when you're around."

Hah! I told *her*. Take *that*, Mrs. Carmichael.

Ringo smiled. "You think? That would make me a lucky charm. It would be cool to counteract the bad mojo with mucho primo vibes."

"Go vibrate," I told him. I stole a look at Mrs. Carmichael. She looked way perplexed. "Now I gotta go."

I turned and noticed the stricken look on Melody's face.

Uh-oh. My efforts to zing Angelina's mom had zanged Melody at the same time.

# CHAPTER 4

# Girl Reporter Finds Her Feet in Her Mouth!

MELODY AND I walked across the field in silence. We got into a rhythm that perfectly matched the refrain clanging in my head: Your big mouth. Your big mouth. Your big mouth.

I snuck a peek at Melody. Her whole face was kind of pinched, and she kept rolling her lips inward. I guess the Ringo-and-Angelina show seriously bugged her.

I sighed. I forgot sometimes that there was all this boy-girl weirdness going on with my friends. Was this something that happened as soon as you entered middle school? Once you graduated from elementary school, did you suddenly graduate to all this other stuff, too?

It wasn't enough that the curriculum got harder and that we went from being the top of the heap to the absolute bottom. No. Add to that big old list the whole girl-boy thing, which seemed to affect everything. Only it never affected everything the same way, at the same time, or to the same degree.

Can you say "stress"?

To me, Ringo was a bud. To Melody, he was crush material. From the looks of things, Angelina might be a player in the mixed-up mix.

Ringo was tough to read. Fact: He liked hanging with Melody. Other fact: He liked all the rahrahs. Newest fact: Angelina seemed to really attract his attention. He also seemed oblivious to why any of this should be a problem. Which was one of his best qualities.

But Melody was bummed.

"That Mrs. Carmichael sure was scary," I said finally. We had left the field and were cruising along the sidewalk.

"Mm-hmm," Melody said.

"This whole cheerleading thing totally escapes me," I said. "Actually, I wish I could escape the cheerleaders."

"It is quite a ridiculous pastime," Melody agreed. "I truly don't understand the appeal it holds for Ringo."

"Well, he does like looking at things from different perspectives," I said. "Upside-down and backwards is definitely a different perspective."

No response.

"The candy-cane squad is probably just a case of temporary insanity," I assured her. "At least I hope so."

"He is capable of so much more than shouting mindless chants," Melody said. "I think it will take a week before I can get the wretched rhymes out of my head."

"I know what you mean," I said. "If I'm not careful I'm going to start chanting my math assignments." I waved my arms over my head like the cheerleaders. "Fractions! Fractions! We've got fractions!" I cheered.

"Do you think I'm fat?"

Whoa! Talk about hairpin turns! I was glad I was walking. If I'd been on my bike, I would've skidded off the road at that sudden change of direction. "What?"

"Do you think I'm fat?" Melody repeated. "Please be honest."

I stopped walking and stared at her. "Of course you're not fat! Why would you even think that?"

Melody turned to face me. She looked serious. "Don't simply tell me what you think I want to hear," she said. "I trust you to tell me the truth."

She had me there. My motto is all truth, all the time. Even if it gets me in trouble. So despite how whacked her question was, I had to take it seriously. "Stand still."

Melody put down the boom box, then stood with her arms held slightly away from her body. I walked all around her, scrutinizing her up and down.

"You are totally not fat," I announced.

To my surprise, she didn't seem relieved. It was as if she didn't believe me. Or that just because *I* didn't think she was fat, that didn't mean she really wasn't.

So I told her again, louder. "Melody," I said firmly. "You are not even the slightest bit fat."

"I am, next to Angelina." She sounded really wistful.

"Please." I rolled my eyes. "Everybody looks fat next to Angelina. She's a teeny-tiny girl. She's practically a lollipop."

"I guess . . . " Melody said.

"Believe me. It's not that you're big, it's that she's so small. Compared to Angelina, Ringo is huge. And I've arm-wrestled him. He's no Schwartzenegger."

Melody sighed. "Maybe that's why Ringo likes her so much."

"Ringo likes everybody," I insisted. "And they

29

have something in common. They both suffer from cheerleading madness."

"Mm."

I picked up the boom box, and we started walking again. I wondered why Melody would think that a boy would like a girl just because he was bigger than her. What a strange way to choose a crush.

Melody was still on this track. I wished I could derail her, but she just kept chugging along to the next station. "Do you think all boys like girls like Angelina?" she asked.

"Huh?" She kept asking bizarre questions that had no answers. I'd have been cut at the two-hundred-dollar mark if this was a game show.

"Do you think we need to be more like Angelina for boys to like us?" Melody persisted.

"What do you mean?" I asked. "You mean do boys only like cheerleaders?"

"No. I mean, little and skinny and blond."

This was a weird concept. "Why would they like us better that way?"

My hand flew up to my straight brown hair. Could there be something wrong with it? Other than always being in my face and getting tangled when I washed it, I mean.

Melody bit her lower lip. With her purple lipliner and long black hair, she looked sort of like an insecure vampire. "It just seems that the most popular girls are those resembling Angelina. Look at the telly. And magazines. And Trumbull."

I scanned my mental player. Could Melody be right? I guess I had never thought about what kind of girls boys like best because I didn't much care. My philosophy is: You are who you are. What you look like is just the package you come in. I inherited that attitude, particularly from Gram. And I truly believe it. Hey—would a chocolate bar be any less chocolate-y if it came in ugly paper?

Melody was still on her own wavelength, though. "Look at Ringo," she persisted.

She had me there. Something about Angelina brought out a different side of Ringo—one I had never seen before. Sort of take charge and protective. I didn't think it was because of how she looked, though. Just the way she was.

Which was the total opposite of me, I realized. Boys were not going to rush to my rescue. Which was just fine with me! I wanted to be out there on the front lines, right in the very heart of danger and excitement. A boy in a clunky suit of armor would only cramp my style.

Then I thought of one boy who might look good riding up on a horse: Tyler McKenzie. But I didn't want him to like me because I was a cream puff needing protection. I wanted him to like me because I'm, well, me!

But would he like me better if I was more like Angelina? Little and blond? I'm on the small side, but I'm not a skinny mini.

My face got hot. Well, if Tyler McKenzie preferred girls like Angelina, then I didn't like him!

Hold on, I scolded myself. You've just had a fight with Tyler, and he isn't even here. All because Melody put these weird ideas in your head.

"It shouldn't be that way," Melody muttered.

"I don't think it is," I assured her.

We got to the corner where she had to peel off and head in a different direction. I handed her back the boom box.

"Ta," she said, absently.

"Quit worrying about Angelina," I told her.

A fresh look of worry crossed her face. Great. She'd thought of something new to obsess over. "Do you think Angelina will be at Megan's sleep-over?" she asked.

I almost dropped my backpack. "What sleep-

32

over?" I didn't mean for it to come out like a squeak. But I was caught off guard.

Megan was having a party?

Melody had just given me my own worry to obsess about.

# Party Plans Go Ka-Plooie!

MELODY LOOKED HORRIFIED. "I thought you knew about the sleepover this weekend. I just assumed—"

I cut her off. "This is the first I heard of it."

"I'm sure it's just an error," Melody said. "Perhaps the invitation got lost in the mail."

"I don't care," I said. "I wouldn't go to a party hosted by Her Royal Pinkness on a dare."

"Well, it would be loads more fun if you *were* there," Melody said. "I don't know that I'd want to go if you don't."

Melody's words made me feel good. For a minute.

"Well, cheers," she said. Not very cheerfully.

"Yeah. Clink-clink," I responded.

I stomped the rest of the way home and

slammed into the house. I banged the door behind me so hard the photos on the wall rattled. I didn't even cringe. I was mad! Furious!

Then I got a hold of myself. It wasn't as if Megan and I were friends or anything. There were times when I can't even stand the Creature from the Pink Lagoon.

"It doesn't matter," I muttered. "It's just a stupid party that I don't want to go to anyway. I should be grateful that I don't have to come up with an excuse not to go."

I charged up the stairs to my room. I dropped my backpack in the corner, then sank down beside the bed.

Why hadn't Megan invited me?

I stood up to shake the green meanies out of me. It didn't work. I grabbed one of my silk Chinese pillows and punched it. Hard. I was knocking the fluff right out of it the way I wanted to knock the fluff out of Megan.

Grr. I punched the pillow harder. Then it hit me: I wasn't mad at Megan. Well, I *was* mad at her. But I was more mad at me—for caring about such a dumb thing.

I stomped back downstairs. I needed a sounding board, a place to vent, a voice of sanity. I needed a dose of Gram.

I've got the coolest grandmother. She's an award-winning journalist who is taking time out from her amazing exciting life to live in Abbington. Why? Me!

My parents are doctors working with this group called Doctors Without Borders. They go to places all over the world, and right now they're in Southeast Asia helping out in the aftermath of a big chemical spill. They're gone for the year.

My brother, Billy, went with them. He's at "that difficult age," in guidance-counselor speak. My parents decided the cultural experience would do him some good. That and close surveillance.

So Gram moved in for the duration, and we both like it that way. She's using the time here to write her memoirs. I'm using it to get journalism tips and quality Gram time.

Uh-oh. The door to the study was closed. The DO NOT DISTURB sign had a desperate quality. How could I tell? Big clue: the three exclamation points scrawled on the Post-it slapped onto the sign.

Gram had been suffering from writer's block. I could relate. I can relate a lot with Gram, and she relates right back. Maybe because we're related.

Just now, though, relating wasn't in my imme-
diate future. *"If I don't talk to someone this minute
I think I'll explode,"* I said aloud. I banged my fists
against my sides.

Duh. Griffin, of course.

Even though Griffin had moved a few hundred
miles away, he was still my best friend. Time for
an online chat.

I charged back up the stairs and logged on.

**To: Thebeast**
**From: Wordpainter**
**Re:**

Talk about writer's block! I couldn't think of
what to say. No way to paint this picture with
words that wouldn't be misunderstood. If I
couldn't figure out why I was so bugged, how
could I explain it to Griffin?

I stared at the screen. I stared at it some more,
waiting for words to come. I stared at it so hard, I
made a message appear through sheer force of
will!

Not really. But an e-mail appeared in my
inbox.

I clicked on it. It was from Griffin.

Call the psychic hot line! It was as if Griffin
knew I was thinking about him. When I'm all in a

bunch, it's great to know that his head is on straight.

**To: Wordpainter**
**From: Thebeast**
**Re: How high is up?**
   Hey. I have a question. How tall is Tyler? And your cartoonist pal, Ringo—how tall is he? What about Gary, your jock nemesis?
   **Griffin**

Why did he want to know the heights of these guys? Was he buying all of them pants?

I sent him an e-mail asking him just that. His answer did not clear things up for me.

**I just wanted to know, ok?**

That sounded a little defensive.

**No, really. What's up? I'm going to keep asking until you tell me. So give up on maintaining silence.**

Okay, so I pressed. It wasn't like Griffin to withhold.

A few minutes passed. Was he going to answer? Why was he being so mysterious?

**You really are the news hound, aren't you? Well, now that you've hounded me, here's the news. I am the shortest boy in my class. Even a lot of girls are taller than me. Is it me? Or am I surrounded by giants?**

I stared at the screen. Here was a weird obsession.

**To: Thebeast**
**From: Wordpainter**
**Re: No worries**
 **You're a giant in my eyes.**
**But I'll research reports of Godzilla and Goliath sightings in your neighborhood.**

**To: Thebeast**
**From: Wordpainter**
**Re: Ha Ha**
 **You're no help.**

That was all he wrote. I felt bad. I guess he really meant it. He was bugged about his height.

He took this tallness thing as seriously as Melody took her phantom-fat issue. So I had to take it seriously, too.

I pictured Griffin. Was he short? I never thought about it. Short, tall, what's the diff? It made a diff to Griff, though.

I guessed that by boy standards, he might be on the shrimpish side. But so what?

I remembered a website I had used for a health class project. I clicked in and found the stats for average heights, along with info about "the adolescent's changing body." I highlighted the part where it said that kids have growth spurts and many don't attain full height until well into their teens. I figured that would make him feel better. He hadn't even made it to twelve yet. He had loads of years to stretch.

**To: Thebeast**
**From: Wordpainter**
**Re: My Bad**

Sorry. It's just that when I think of you I don't think about whether you're tall or short or thin or fat or any of that stuff. I just think of you as my best bud. So read the attachment and let sanity prevail!

I hit Send and hoped he'd feel better. On the other hand, I was still feeling like burned crumbs. Glancing at the chart I'd just sent to Griffin didn't improve my mood any. According to these statistics, I was totally average.

Oh joy.

# Girls Vow to Stick to Green-Slime Diet!

I WOKE UP the next day in a deep-blue funk. I barely spoke at breakfast and wasn't very hungry. I just crammed in a few Pop-tarts and left it at that.

Gram was all fuzzy, so my mood didn't register. Sleeplessness seemed to be a side effect of writer's block. Normally, I'd get a minitalk about eating a healthier breakfast. Gram's as much into junk food as I am, but she makes me down some fruit and veggies on a daily basis. Maybe today she decided strawberry Pop-tarts qualified as a serving of fruit.

She had the presence of mind to mutter "Milk. Vitamins. OJ." Then she drifted off again.

I trudged to school. Normally I'm that weird kid who likes showing up at school. Not that I'm all that into classes. It's *Real News* that recharges my batteries, scouting for stories and generally basking in the newsroom atmosphere.

Last year, Trumbull didn't even have a newspaper. Canceled for lack of interest. It took us feisty sixth graders to resurrect it, and it's been a big success—thanks to me. Okay—and Gary Williams, Toni Velez, Ringo and our faculty advisor, Mr. Baxter.

Oh yeah. And that traitorous Megan O'Connor.

Today I avoided the office. I wanted to put off seeing Megan as long as I could.

First stop: my locker. As I trudged down the hall, my heart sped up a little. There was a note sticking out of the crack of my locker door. I'd recognize that pink stationery anywhere. My feet hurried along to match my new heart rate. Was it an invitation? Had Megan invited me after all?

I stopped in my tracks. "Wait a sec," I murmured. Had Melody said something to Megan last night? I didn't want a pity invitation. That would be worse than no invitation at all.

I bit my lip and snatched the envelope. It wasn't an invitation. Megan wanted us all to meet at the *Real News* office after school so she could run some ideas by us.

Did I feel like a total dork or what? My mood

took an express ride down into my green Converse high-tops.

It was obvious. Megan thought of me only as a newspaper reporter, not as a friend. Fine by me. That's all I wanted to be, anyway. I crumpled up the pink paper and tossed it into the wastebasket on my way into homeroom.

Which reminded me: I needed to start thinking about next week's issue. Ms. Tiwell, one of the teachers, had just announced her early retirement. The rumor was that she had made a killing in the stock market. That could be an interesting profile.

Then there was Angelina. Could she really be the target of some serious wacko? If she was, that would make a great story. But that was a big if.

The bell rang, and I raced to the Terminator's math class. I had forced myself to do the optional problems last night as a way to get my mind off Megan. I didn't want to cancel out the extra credits by getting a tardy mark.

I slid into my seat just as the late bell rang. For a moment I understood the appeal of sliding into home base.

I pulled out my notebook and gazed at the chalkboard. I was going to forget all about Megan's stupid party. I was going to learn all about exponents.

I chewed on my pencil. I don't want to go to Megan's party, I reminded myself. Think of who her friends are. It would be like Megan to the tenth power.

Why wouldn't she invite me, though? That was a puzzler. All morning I kept running it over and over in my head. Had I done something to offend her?

Well, duh. Practically every day. But it never seemed to really bother her. Maybe it did, I thought. Maybe she'd reached the breaking point with me and couldn't take it anymore. Maybe I should work harder to keep my mouth shut and be nice to her.

Get real! Why should I change myself? She could take me or leave me—the two-faced traitor. But it was clear she didn't want to include me in her non–*Real News* life.

Not that I wanted to orbit in Megan's cotton candy universe. I didn't think I could take that much sweetness without winding up with severe cavities.

Concentrate, Casey, I told myself. Get off this Megan mania and back to what actually matters.

In social studies I scrawled some notes for possible stories:

Can kids play the stock market? Can the soon-to-be ex-teacher Ms. Tiwell give some tips? Maybe start up a stock market club. Investing in our future?

This story might tip dangerously close to advanced math class. Boring and hardly cutting edge.

I'll tell you what cut deep: this underhanded way Megan had of squeezing me out. If she had a problem with me, she should tell me to my face instead of playing these dumb cold-shoulder games.

No, no, no! I should consider myself lucky! Just imagine what that party would be like! Did I really want to be trapped overnight with Megan and her Megan clones?

Still, Melody was going, and she was kind of the anti-Megan. They'd yin-yang each other into a safety zone.

Aaaaggghhh! Instead of being my usual motormouth self, I was suffering from motor*brain*. And it was operating in overdrive. I could feel steam blasting out of my ears.

That's what it was like all morning. It was a total relief when the bell rang and it was time for lunch. I would distract myself by trying to survive today's menu.

I pushed through the cafeteria doors.

## MIDDLE SCHOOLERS OVERCOME BY SERIOUS STINK!

Was that a story? Nah. Bad cafeteria food was old news.

I spotted Ringo sitting with the rah-rahs. One thing I've noticed is that the only times kids from different grades mix it up are when they're in the same club or on the same team. Otherwise everyone sticks pretty closely inside their grade boundaries.

I carried my tray toward the table of Frosted Cheerios. After all, Ringo was a true friend. I could be a true friend too. I could suck it up and put up with the pep-eronis for his sake.

"Hi Ringo," I greeted him.

"Casey." He pulled out the empty chair beside him. "Sit."

I was about to scoot into the chair when my brain processed the sight in front of me.

"Are you being punished for something?" I

asked. "Or is this one of those gross hazing rituals you hear about in sports?"

Five pairs of eyes blinked at me.

"Hello? The menu?" I was still gripping my lunch tray, so I tipped my head at the table.

I recognized the food items they had piled up in the center of the table, but it didn't add up to lunch. A head of cabbage. A can of tomato soup. A can of cream of mushroom soup. A can of beef broth. Plastic cups of water. A plastic cup filled with lemon slices. A grapefruit. "Blecch" was the only word that came to mind.

"It's the cabbage soup diet," Marcy explained, as if I would know what that meant. "It's the total bomb."

"Looks more like the total barf," I commented. I plopped down in the empty seat next to Ringo.

"Models drink water with lemon slices." Samantha continued the tour through the twisted food-pyramid. "So we thought we would try it."

"Grapefruit makes you burn extra calories," Tara added. "So you actually lose weight by eating." She gushed as if it was the best discovery since Columbus landed.

"We thought if we all went on a diet together we wouldn't cheat," Samantha explained. She beamed at me.

I thought any second they'd start a cheer:

Two! Four! Six! Eight!
Lose weight! It's great!
Skipping chocolate is our fate!

I looked around the table. They were totally nuts. Not one of these girls needed to be on a diet, and if Ringo lost any weight he could slip through a fax machine.

"Are you really going to eat that stuff?" I asked. No one seemed to have touched any of the food yet.

The cheerleaders all studied the food. "I have a question," Ringo said. "Maybe I'm missing something, but isn't the cabbage supposed to be *in* the soup?"

"I didn't have time to make the soup," Marcy explained. "Besides, it would be hard to cart in a big vat of soup."

"We have all the ingredients," Samantha agreed. "It all gets mixed up together after we eat it anyway, right?"

I noticed that Tara, Angelina and Ringo looked a little dubious. Maybe there were a few brains in the bunch after all.

Marcy held up a can opener. She punctured

the top of the can of cream of mushroom soup and stuck in a straw.

"We have to drink it cold?" Tara asked. "Straight from the can?"

Marcy glared at Tara. "You want to be on the diet, don't you?"

"You realize you're all insane, right?" I asked.

Marcy looked at me with a face full of pity. Like I was a dodo bent on destroying my life by—gasp—eating actual food.

Marcy took a sip of the cream of mushroom soup. I could see her working hard not to gag. "It is so important that we cheerleaders set the standard," she choked out.

I raised one eyebrow. I didn't like the idea that Marcy was setting some kind of standard for girls at Trumbull. Who put her in charge?

"With the competition coming up, we really need to get in shape," Samantha added, taking the can of soup from Marcy. "Appearance is a major category." She took a sip and made a face, then handed the can to Tara.

"I bet it is," I commented. She just confirmed my opinion of cheerleaders as decorative items. Worse—they decorated something equally trivial: sports events. They were a sideline to a sideline.

"Do you remember Penny Tosher?" Tara

asked. She took a sip from the soup can and passed it across to Angelina.

Marcy and Samantha, both seventh graders, nodded solemnly.

"Who's Penny Tosher?" Angelina asked. I noticed she didn't take a swig, but passed the can on. Smart girl.

"She was in line to be the next head cheerleader last year," Tara explained. Tara was in the eighth grade and had been on the squad her first two years at Trumbull. "Penny couldn't keep her weight down. She got booted off the squad for it."

Wow. That seemed harsh.

"Marcy, open up the tomato soup. I love gazpacho," Ringo said. "I bet it's pretty much the same thing."

"All right." Marcy bcamcd at him.

"What do you think of this diet idea?" I asked Ringo. Surely Ringo would represent the voice of reason. Which was a scary idea, but under the circumstances quite possible.

Ringo shrugged. "I'm usually on the bottom of the pyramid. The lighter the girls are, the easier it is."

Okay, the logic was weird, but at least it was practical.

"Besides," he continued. "I like trying new ways of eating. Food is like a universal language.

I wonder what the melting pot tastes like."

Ringo picked up the grapefruit and began peeling it.

"Hey!" Some of the juice had squirted right into my eye. "Watch it. That's a lethal weapon."

Tara leaned in and lowered her voice. "Someone should tell that girl those pants fit her in a former life."

Marcy and Samantha giggled. I glanced over to see who Tara was talking about. An eighth-grade girl was moving between the tables. She was kind of hefty, but that didn't seem like a reason to make fun of her.

"Look at that," Samantha murmured. She tipped her head toward the table behind us. "Don't look," she whispered.

I hate that. Why did she tell us to look if she didn't want us to?

Marcy dropped her fork. As she bent down to pick it up, she scoped out the table. "Eww."

"What?" I demanded. Was someone picking boogers or something?

"Caroline Gidreau," Marcy whispered. "She swore to me she was going to go on a diet."

"She could use it," Samantha said.

"Check out her tray," Tara added. "Lasagna *and* bread *and* potatoes? Plus dessert and chocolate milk?"

"How can she do that?" Samantha said.

I glanced down at my tray. What did they think of my selections?

I wasn't going to let a bunch of rah-rahs stand between me and my chocolate cake. It's one of the few things they actually get right in the cafeteria.

I took a forkful and brought it to my mouth. I have never felt so scrutinized while I ate since I choked on a mouthful of beets at my aunt Denise's house. All of the cheerleaders—except Ringo—gazed at me sadly.

I popped the piece into my mouth. Ahhhhhhh. Chocolate. Frosting. Excellent. The route to sanity.

I checked the expressions again. Hm. Now some of them seemed downright envious. That made a lot more sense. Maybe they really were human.

They all held out their hands to Ringo for sections of grapefruit. A sad sight.

"I have to stop by my gym locker before my next class," Angelina said. "Only after everything that's happened, it gives me the willies. I'm afraid of what I might find."

"I'll go with you," Ringo offered.

That set off a round of giggles. "Ringo! You can't go with her," Marcy said. "It's the *girls'* locker room."

53

"How sweet, Angelina," Tara added. "You have your very own hero."

"I could go for a hero sandwich," Ringo said. "This cabbage soup diet leaves me with a dino-sized appetite."

"Depending on the dino, you might have to go total vegan," Angelina said.

"I'll go with you." I jumped up. I wanted to find out if there were any legs to this stalker story. If it wasn't going to work, I needed to start scouting for another front-page topic.

"Really? Thanks." Angelina pushed away from the table.

I took a last bite of my chocolate cake and stood.

Ringo drank down some more soup. He winced and downed some water. He gargled and swished the water around in his mouth. "I need to hit my locker, too," he said.

I figured he had a stash of granola bars in his locker. He'd need something to kill the taste of cold mushroom glop.

"See you at practice," Angelina told the remaining rah-rahs.

"Bye, Angelina. Bye, Ringo," the other girls chimed. They all giggled.

Ringo and Angelina didn't seemed fazed by

the teasing. They just shook their heads and grinned. I wondered how Melody would feel if she had witnessed this scene.

"Bye, Casey," I muttered to myself. I felt invisible. Maybe it was because everyone was looking at the chunk of chocolate cake I had left on the plate. Would they cave?

## CRAZED BY LACK OF CHOCOLATE, CHEERLEADERS BATTLE OVER LEFTOVERS! "Not a pretty sight," Casey Smith reports.

We left the cafeteria and walked toward the girls' locker room. Well, *I* walked. I don't know what those two were doing.

"T-rex," Angelina cried. They both bent their arms and brought their hands up to their necks, scrunching them into claws. They roared and stalked down the hall.

"Pterodactyl," Angelina ordered.

Now they flapped their arms as if they had heavy wings.

"Chubbawaxosaur," Ringo called.

Angelina socked his arm. "There's no such thing!"

"No wonder the dinosaurs are extinct," I muttered, and walked past them.

55

Angelina fell into step beside me. "Actually, there's a whole bunch of different theories about why the dinosaurs became extinct."

"Is serious goofiness one of the reasons?" I asked.

"I think goofiness would be adaptive," Angelina replied. "Though I guess it wouldn't help if you were totaled by a meteorite."

Huh? All I did was make a crack, and she turned it into some kind of theory. There was something going on under those yellow waves. A cheerleader with brains? Wow. Between Ringo and Angelina I might have to rethink my cheerleader worldview.

Bummer.

We arrived at the door to the girls' locker room.

"Okay, dude," I told Ringo. "This is where we separate the boys from the girls."

"You want me to hang around?" he asked.

"Nah," I told him. "We can take it from here."

"See you at practice," Angelina said.

Ringo made a dino-face and roared. Then he took off down the hall.

"Let's check out your locker," I said.

We pushed through the swinging doors.

And I thought the smell in the cafeteria was overwhelming.

# NEW CHEMICAL WARFARE!
## Smelly Socks and Wet Towels Studied for Military Use

"It's over here," Angelina said.

She led me between the rows of lockers. I spotted a stray sock here, a notepad there. Some hair scrunchies. A copper bracelet.

Angelina faltered. She looked as if she might faint.

"Angelina, you didn't eat anything at lunch, did you?" I scolded her.

She didn't answer. She just pointed a trembling hand toward her locker.

I let out a gasp. Something was dripping out of the crack of the locker door. Something red.

Something that looked a lot like blood.

# Gruesome Discovery in Girls' Locker Room!

ANGELINA CLUTCHED MY arm. "Wh-what do you think is in there?"

I took a deep breath. I mustered up all the guts I had—which were in shorter supply than I'd expected.

It's not like I thought there was a severed head in there. Not really. But whatever was dripping onto the floor was seriously gross.

I approached the locker. "What's the combination?" I asked.

"Two turns to the left, twenty-three . . ." Angelina began.

I reached for the dial. To my surprise, as soon as I tugged on it, the lock opened.

I glanced at Angelina.

"I swear I locked it," she said.

I took another one of those deep breaths that are supposed to be so calming.

Note to self: Breathing thing a myth!

I swung open the locker. Angelina let out a squeak.

A Barbie in a cheerleader's outfit hung from a hook inside. It looked like it was covered in blood.

I have to admit it. The chocolate cake from lunch did a serious herkie in my stomach.

See? I was paying attention during Ringo's practice.

Angelina sank down onto the floor. She leaned against the row of lockers and covered her face with her hands.

"Creepy," I murmured.

"Who could hate me so much?" she whispered. It was as if she couldn't bear to say the words out loud.

"My question is, how did this person get into your locker?"

Angelina brought her hands down and stared at me. Her green eyes looked even bigger than normal. "My sneakers were in my locker, too. And my cheer book."

"Who else knows the combination?" I asked. "We figure that out, and we've got your perp."

"My what?" Angelina asked.

I waved my hands around. "You know. Perp. Perpetrator. Culprit."

Angelina stared at me blankly.

"Meanie," I said. Sheesh. Didn't she watch cop shows? Read newspapers?

Angelina hugged her knees to her chest. She had to be really upset. You couldn't pay me to sit on the locker room floor. Wet. Damp. Athlete's foot. Eww.

I sat on a bench and leaned toward her, elbows on my knees. "Think, Angelina. Who besides you knows the combination to your lock?"

"I've never told it to anyone," she insisted.

"Well, somehow somebody has gotten into your supposedly locked locker." I cocked my head to one side. "Are you positive about locking it?"

She set her mouth in a firm straight line. "Even if I forgot to lock it once, I couldn't have forgotten all those other times."

She bounced her chin on her knees a few times. She stopped and looked up at me. "You know what? I wrote my combination in my notebook. In case I forgot it."

I wondered what she'd do if she forgot the combination *after* she locked her notebook inside. But I let it slide.

"It's possible someone found it out that way. Bring a new lock tomorrow."

Angelina nodded.

I got up and took the blood-smeared doll out of the locker. I handled it carefully: 1) I didn't want to get blood on me. 2) The doll was evidence.

I held the Barbie by the hair. "I don't think it's real blood," I said.

I didn't sound too convincing. I mean, I really didn't think it was real, but who knew?

I laid the Barbie doll on the bench. "Check if anything's missing. I'm going to do a quick search."

I figured whoever did this applied the "blood" after the Barbie was already hanging in the locker. Otherwise it was just too messy. We'd have seen a red trail.

I went over to the garbage can and peeked in. "Aha!" I pulled some plastic tubes from the garbage. "Fake blood."

I darted back to Angelina. She still stood there, staring into the locker.

I dangled the fake-blood tubes at Angelina. "See, it's not real."

"That's a clue, isn't it?" Angelina asked.

"Kind of." I examined the packets. They were the kind of goop you buy for Halloween and stuff. You could get them at the party store at the mall. Nothing special.

Then I checked out Barbie. "Is this a standard

Barbie? Or did someone have to make the costume?"

Angelina nodded. "I have that one. It's not rare or anything."

"So any kid who knew your combination could have managed this."

"Any *girl*," Angelina pointed out.

"At least we've narrowed down the suspects." I grinned at Angelina, trying to lighten the mood.

She smiled back, though awfully weakly. She was obviously shaken. Who wouldn't be, finding a bloody Barbie in her locker? Especially since the doll looked like her. Angelina had the same blond hair. Same big green eyes and perky expression. Minus the humongo chest and the permanently arched feet, of course.

This stank worse than stinky cheese. And it didn't smell like a harmless prank. This was mean.

"Can you think of anyone who you know is mad at you?" I asked her.

"I don't think so." Angelina's pale brows furrowed together. "You'd have to be super mad to do something like this."

She was right. This was extreme. Bordering on sicko.

"Do you think it's someone who wants me

off the squad?" Angelina suggested. "Everything seems connected to the cheerleading competition."

"Maybe." The perpetrator might be sending a message, since Angelina's regular locker had been left alone. Her books, her homework were never touched—just the stuff related to cheerleading.

I didn't want to decide too soon, though. I knew that it was important for a reporter to keep an open mind. Otherwise you could miss important clues. "The cheerleading link might simply be the easiest way to get at you," I told her.

"Oh." She seemed a little disappointed that I hadn't jumped at her competition theory. She probably wanted the quickest route to the solution.

I wondered what would happen once Angelina changed her lock. Would the culprit give up? Or would they just find new ways to torment her?

I confess: My next thought was that this was excellent story material. Front-page stuff. Exciting, especially if I was the one to catch the culprit.

Then I had another thought: I wondered if the person who did this would stop at dolls. The pranks were escalating. Could Angelina be in real danger?

# Who Killed Barbie?

THE BELL RANG. Angelina nearly jumped out of her skin. Then she let out a nervous, embarrassed laugh.

"Sorry," she said. "This all has me a little teetery."

She picked up the Barbie and threw it into the garbage.

"Angelina!" I scolded. "Don't throw that away. It's evidence!" I went over to the garbage can, fished around and pulled out the doll.

Eww. Used tissue stuck to the fake blood. I made a quick exception to the evidence rule. I dropped the doll back into the garbage.

"You have to report this," I said as we left the locker room to get to class.

Angelina stopped walking. "I can't!" she said. "This person is already mad at me. That will only make them madder." She was getting kind of hysterical. Her voice was reaching a frequency only dogs could hear.

I tried to talk some sense into her. "It's possible this person is dangerous."

"I'll think about it, I promise. But swear you won't say anything yet."

I narrowed my eyes at her.

"Casey," she pleaded.

"Okay," I grumbled. "For now."

Angelina's predicament kept me preoccupied all afternoon. Which was good because it kept me from obsessing about Megan and her party. In fact, I'd forgotten all about it—until I walked into the *Real News* office after school.

"Hi, Casey," Megan chirped from her spot in front of the computer.

Seeing her coordinated pink-and-white outfit with matching pink ballet flats and pink barrettes brought it all back in a rush. Slam-dunked me like one of Gary's rare baskets.

Afraid of what I would say, I kept my mouth shut and sat at our polka-dotted table, Dalmatian Station.

Just act like you don't care a Fig Newton about that dumb party, I ordered myself. Don't even bring it up.

Where was everybody? Megan's note had requested everyone's presence. I wished Gary, Toni and Ringo would hurry up and get here already. Megan was bound to notice my out-of-character silence.

Besides, the only way I could keep from blurting out something about the party was by biting the inside of my cheek.

"Casey, is something wrong?" Megan asked.

Keeping my teeth in place, I murmured, "Uh uh."

Ouch. That smarted. I've got sharp teeth.

I didn't let myself turn around. It would be much too hard to resist the urge to muss her up.

"Casey?"

"Mm."

"Seriously, is something wrong?"

"No, Madame Inquisition. Nothing is wrong!"

So much for maintaining neutrality. Even *I* could hear the icicles dangling from my frosty tone.

"If you don't want to come to my party," Megan snapped, "just tell me. You don't have to act all snotty about it!"

I whirled around in my chair. "Me? Acting snotty?"

"Yes." Megan crossed her arms over her chest. Which was a relief, because it blotted out the cutesy butterflies floating across her shirt.

Wait a sec. Something she said didn't make any sense. "How can I tell you I don't want to come to your dumb old party when I wasn't even invited?"

Hah! I waited to see her wriggle out of that one.

Megan's face crinkled up in confusion. "What do you mean? I sent you an invitation. Didn't you get it?"

I studied her. Was she telling the truth? Or was she just covering because she knew I had heard about the party?

It would be totally unlike Megan to lie. So what had happened to the invitation?

Toni Velez, staff photographer, bounded into the room. She waved a pink envelope, making her bangle bracelets jingle, jangle, jingle. "My mom said it's cool," she told Megan. "I'll be there."

"Oh, I'm so pleased." Megan's face turned all smiley.

I gaped at Toni. She was invited to Megan's party? And she was actually going?

Of course, Toni respected Megan. I guess she

even liked her. But I didn't think a sleepover in Pinksville was Toni's style.

"Oh, by the way." Toni put her camera on the table and reached into her backpack. "This is for you."

She tossed a folded paper at me. There, in pink and purple, was my name on a party invitation, complete with the little curlicues Megan adds whenever possible.

"How did *you* get it?" I asked.

"It was squished inside my envelope," Toni explained.

"The glitter glue must have stuck the invitations together," Megan said. "Well, that mystery is solved." Looking relieved, she beamed at me. "You see, Casey? Of course I invited you."

"Oh. Uh. Thanks." I had just realized something. Now I'd actually have to go.

"We have two minutes and fifteen seconds," Ringo was telling Gary as they walked into the newsroom together. "Got that? Two minutes. Fifteen seconds. That's it."

"I heard you, Ringo, the first seven times." Gary grabbed his baseball cap and flipped it backward.

"Two minutes and fifteen seconds to make it or break it." Ringo hopped up onto the table and crossed his legs. "That's not long enough to say hello, much less do a whole routine."

"Megan," Gary said in a pleading tone. "Please. Can someone else cover the cheerleaders' meet? Ringo's anxiety is contagious."

"Make it part of the story," Megan said sweetly. "It ups the drama."

"Maybe I should have tried out for the drama club instead," Ringo muttered. "They give you more than two minutes and fifteen seconds, don't they?"

"Can we get this meeting started?" Toni asked, pulling her camera strap out from under Ringo's thigh.

"Sorry," Ringo said. "I need to zenify."

Ringo shut his eyes and placed his hands palms up on his knees. Then his gray eyes opened again.

"Oh! I have something I wanted to say." He fiddled around in his many pockets until he found a crumpled wad of paper. "I just wanted to thank everyone here," he read from the paper, "for making it possible for me to pursue an anti-gravity dream, work on achieving serious air-space, and memorize additional cheers. Thank you."

Toni looked at me. I looked at Gary. Gary looked at Megan. Megan grinned, then gave a quick nod. "You're welcome," we chimed in unison.

Ringo grinned. "Awesome. A *Real News* cheer. Coolness."

"Now that Ringo has made his speech," Megan declared, "I'd like to talk about an idea I had for the next issue."

"Already? I'm not ready to pitch a story," I complained. "We usually do story meetings on Monday."

"It's just that this idea would affect those stories," Megan explained. "So I wanted to run it by you all first."

"So, hit us with it already." Toni snapped her gum. "I've got places, people, yadda yadda."

Megan folded her hands in front of her. "For this week's JAM column," she said, "I thought I'd concentrate on a single theme. And it struck me that we could do some stories to go along with it."

A whole warm and squishy issue? Ick. Bad idea. I said, "I don't know—"

"What's the topic?" Toni asked.

I didn't need to know the topic. If it was for Megan's warm and fuzzy advice column, I already knew I wouldn't like it.

Marshmallow media is so not me.

"I'd like to write about body image," Megan declared. "You know, worries about looks, weight, self-esteem, that kind of stuff."

Gary looked totally disgusted. "A whole issue

of that junk? Isn't that kind of extreme?"

"Well, this is why I wanted your input." Megan had her pen poised to take down notes. "It's just that I've been getting mail on this topic since day one. Kids thinking they're too ugly, too fat, too thin, too short, too tall. It seems to really hit home."

"I've heard the refrain myself," Toni commented. "It is topic number one."

"I've done some preliminary research." Megan's voice grew serious. "The information is scary. Problems with body image can result in serious eating disorders. The most frightening fact is that they are on the rise and starting younger and younger." She paused and held each one of us in her gaze. "As young as us, or even younger."

We were all silent. I didn't know what kind of impact Megan's speech had on the others, but bells were going off in my head.

Usually this kind of story isn't my speed. It borders on the touchy-feely-crunchy territory I work really hard to avoid. But this subject had some relevance.

I might not have thought so last week. But hadn't I spent all of lunch today listening to twigs talk about their weirdo weight-loss diet? I also rewound the conversation with Melody yesterday.

A perfectly normal—well, average—well, a totally *cool* girl worrying that she was fat.

I also flashed on Marcy's comment that the rah-rahs were dieting because the cheerleaders set the standards.

What standards? For weight? Looks? Who made these standards the cheerleaders felt they must uphold—and we should all conform to?

That gave me my angle. "We should write about how people get these ideas of how they're supposed to look in the first place. Why all these girls feel bad about themselves as a result. We can expose the whole media image of beauty that's being shoved down our throats."

Megan looked stunned. I guess I'd never agreed to a story idea of hers so quickly. But this story would have a wider scope than Megan's usual cheese.

"Girl, I think the idea is awesome." Toni nodded her head so vigorously that her wild curls bounced. "Someone should expose the pressures on us chickadees."

"The entire newspaper will be girly," Gary objected. "Even my sports coverage, thanks to the cheerleaders' competition. You know, boys go to this school, too."

"This issue affects boys, too," Megan pointed out.

Toni laughed. "Girlfriend, you got that right. Boys can be even more vain than girls. I tell you, my sister's boyfriend is always checking his hair, cruising himself in mirrors."

"Hair is important," Ringo said. "It helps keep our brains warm." He quickly sketched one of his Simon cartoons:

Simon Says: I'm having a seriously Bad Hair Day

"Not just hair," I said. I nodded toward Ringo. "Even boys go on diets. Just ask Ringo."

"Get out," Toni exclaimed. She stared at Ringo. "Are you whacked?" Her eyes narrowed as Ringo reached into his box of granola bars.

"That's your diet?"

Ringo shrugged. "Marcy stopped me in the hall. We're changing diets."

"The cabbage soup thing wasn't a hit?" I asked.

Ringo munched the cookie. "Nope. I just wish I could remember if we decided on all cookies or no cookies."

"I vote for all cookies," I said.

"This whole diet thing is hard to track," Ringo added. "We keep switching. Tomorrow is bananas and potatoes day."

"What a combo." My stomach flip-flopped again.

"Dieting is only part of the problem," Megan said. I thought she was trying to get us back on track. "There was an article in a major newspaper about how the new action figures are making boys feel inadequate."

"Poor them," Toni scoffed. "As if they should compare themselves to plastic dudes like Superman and GI Joe. Like they're real role models."

"Some boys even take growth hormones to make themselves bigger and taller," Megan continued. "That's really dangerous."

"Why would they go that far?" I asked.

"Height is a major deal for dudes," Gary admitted. "Not for me, though," he added hastily.

"You're tall already," Ringo pointed out.

Oh man. Another bell clanged in my head.

Griffin. Was this the hidden meaning behind his weird message yesterday?

"Kids shouldn't think they need to be different from how they are," I said. "It's terrible that kids get held up to some weird standard, so that then if they can't measure up, they feel bad about themselves."

"It's hard to have twenty-twenty vision when you're trying to see yourself," Ringo mused. He popped the rest of the granola bar into his mouth.

"So you're up for this?" Megan asked us. "You think it's a good idea to tie the articles together this way?"

"Do they *all* have to have this angle?" Gary asked. "When I cover the games this week, do I have to interview players to see how they feel about their bodies? Or can I just report the scores and the moves?"

"You can do your usual bang-up job with the sports coverage," Megan assured him.

I tapped my pencil against my front teeth. "Hm."

Megan glanced at me. "I'm into this idea," I assured her. "But nothing sounds like front-page material."

I hoped my Angelina story would be that front-pager. Until I knew for sure, I wasn't going to say anything.

"You may be right," Megan admitted. "We might have to go off theme for our front page. We can make our final decisions as we get closer to deadline."

I planned for that front-page spot to be mine . . . but time would tell.

"I've got to split," Ringo said. "To do splits."

"I have to go, too," Gary grumbled. "I need to talk to the coach and the cheerleaders about the next meet."

"I'll take some shots to go with the story," Toni suggested. The three of them traipsed out together.

"Do you still need help with the layout?" I asked. I was itching to get to practice. I wondered if there'd be any new trouble for Angelina.

"Nah," Megan said. "It's in good shape. You can take off."

"Great." I gathered up my stuff.

Megan beamed at me. I swear, it was as if she had lightbulbs inside instead of guts. "I'm so glad we cleared up the birthday party mix-up. It would have been terrible if you thought you weren't invited."

"No biggie. Later."

I rushed out of the newsroom to the girls' locker room. I skidded to a stop. I thought they must have just waxed the floors, because I slid a little.

I just realized. I had a brand-new crisis.

What was I going to get Megan for her birthday?

# Pit-Bull Mom Bites Innocent Bystander!

How would I ever figure out a present for Megan? I hated shopping in the first place. In the second place, the stores catering to Megan's taste made my skin crawl.

In the third place, I was totally clueless about what she'd like. I knew the general feel—rainbows, kittens, things that sparkled. But how to translate that into an actual present?

You got me.

Worry about Megan's gift later, I told myself. Right now I had a perp to catch.

I dashed into the girls' locker room and nearly collided with a large girl coming out of the bathroom. "Watch it," she snapped.

I took a few steps backward. I recognized the stringy hair and sneer. It was Angelina's older sister, Lauren. She looked like she was going to deck me.

Maybe she just always looked like that.

"Wh-what are you doing in here?" I asked.

She crossed her thick arms over chest. "In the bathroom? Take a guess." She turned and stomped away.

"Whatever," I muttered.

What a nasty girl, I thought. Her whole MO was the total opposite of Angelina's. Who was nowhere in sight. Practice must have started.

I hurried into the gym. Instead of jumping around making me dizzy, the squad had gathered in a clump in front of Coach Seltzer.

"I don't know who is doing this, or why," Coach Seltzer lectured. "But I don't like it one bit."

I sidled up next to Angelina. "What's going on?" I whispered.

"The janitor found the bloody Barbie and showed it to Coach Seltzer," Angelina explained.

Busted. I wondered what would happen now.

"I understand sometimes these things seem funny," Coach Seltzer continued. "But they can easily get out of hand. I want this to stop now. Anyone I catch pulling stunts will be suspended from the squad."

A murmur rose among the Cheerios. They

sent each other suspicious glances. If the culprit was among them, she sure wasn't revealing herself. Only now everyone was going to be on the lookout, including Coach Seltzer.

Would that help my investigation or hurt it?

Uh-oh. Incoming. Mrs. Carmichael strode toward the group. "We never pulled pranks like this when I was on the squad," she declared.

Obviously, she had heard Coach Seltzer's whole speech.

"I think there's a lot of jealousy in this group," Mrs. Carmichael said, surveying the cheerleaders. "You just have to deal with the fact that none of you are as good as Angelina." She gave the group a fako sympathy smile. "Not everyone can be the star. That doesn't mean that each and every one of you isn't important."

Angelina looked totally mortified. The cheerleaders squirmed uncomfortably.

Something seemed to catch Mrs. Carmichael's eagle eyes. I glanced at the bleachers behind me.

The black girl with the braids from yesterday was back. She had a smirk on her face, as if she thought the whole thing was a big joke.

"You!" Mrs. Carmichael pointed at the girl. "You're not supposed to be here!"

Huh? I nearly got whiplash as my head swung back and forth between the mysterious stranger and the deranged pit-bull mom. I wondered who the girl was—and why she had Mrs. Carmichael so freaked.

The girl crossed her arms over her ample chest and glared. She sucked in her cheeks as if she was sucking on a lemon. She didn't say a word.

Mrs. Carmichael took a few steps toward the bleachers. "Was that prank your handiwork? That's just what you want, isn't it? To tear this squad apart."

Wow. This was turning into a front-page story right before my very eyes—and my pen!

# Spy Strikes Back!

I HAD TO give it to the girl—whoever she was. Mrs. Carmichael didn't make her blink.

Instead, the girl stood up and put her hands on her curvy hips. "It's a free country," the girl retorted. "I've got a right to be anywhere I want to be."

She reached down and picked up her backpack and slung the straps over one shoulder. "And just so you know—I don't care if your daughter is on the squad or not. None of them are that good!"

The girl stalked away.

"You better not come here to spy anymore!" Mrs. Carmichael shouted after her. She whirled around and faced off with Coach Seltzer again.

"That girl should be reported!" Mrs. Carmichael said.

"For what?" Coach Seltzer asked.

"She was trespassing. Spying! And she's probably the one who has been tormenting Angelina!"

I scribbled frantically. At this rate, Mrs. Carmichael was going to have my whole story written for me! I suddenly decided she was my best friend. What a source.

"Why do you think she's spying?" I asked. "Do you know who she is?"

To my surprise, she actually answered me. "I don't know her name," Mrs. Carmichael explained. "She's a cheerleader for Perkins Day School."

I recognized the name of a fancy private school nearby. Sometimes our teams competed with their teams.

"How do you know?" I asked. I wanted to verify all my sources before I put this baby to bed.

"I've seen them before," Mrs. Carmichael explained. "I've gone to their meets. They're our toughest rivals in this competition."

"Ha!" Angelina's sister, Lauren, barked behind me. I guessed that barking thing ran in the family. "So you spied on them, huh, Mom?" Lauren said. "That's real mature."

Mrs. Carmichael narrowed her eyes and shot daggers at Lauren. "I was doing important research."

"How is that any different from what that girl was doing here?" Lauren demanded.

Wow. Lauren really talked back to her mom.

"Lauren." Mrs. Carmichael used a tone that made even Lauren clam up. They must teach that tone in parent school.

I glanced at Angelina. I couldn't tell if she was more upset by all the pranks pulled on her or by her mom's behavior. She had kept it together for the worst of the incidents: the bloody Barbie doll. She was more grossed out than upset by the eggy sneakers. Now she was flat-out crying.

If I had Mrs. Carmichael for a mom, I'd cry, too. It was also possible that Angelina was at her breaking point.

Which could just be what the perp wanted.

# Cheerleader No Longer Cheerful!

I COULD JUST see Monday's headlines:

### CULPRIT SNAGGED IN HALLS OF TRUMBULL!
### Reporter Casey Smith Makes School Safe Again

My news radar buzzed full tilt. I just wished it was loud enough to drown out the annoying shouts of "Go team go!"

I took their advice. I went.

It wasn't until I sat down to dinner with Gram that it hit me. I had never made it to the mall!

When could I go? I twirled my spaghetti around my fork. Today was already Friday. The party was tomorrow night. I had investigating to do, too.

Of course, I could go to the mall *before*

cheerleader practice. I slurped a long noodle into my mouth. If Gram drove me, I could make it in plenty of time *and* weasel some gift advice from Gram while I was at it.

"Gram," I said. I licked the tomato sauce from the corners of my mouth. It's amazing how good food from a jar can taste. "Can we do a run to the mall tomorrow?"

"Mm-hmm."

Strange. She didn't even squawk or ask questions. Normally she would be surprised if I suggested a mall crawl.

Must be that writer's block. I wondered if I could make this work for me. "Can I have your dessert?" I'd seen two plastic-wrapped brownies on the kitchen counter.

"Mm-hmm."

My eyebrow raised. How far could I take this? "So, Gram. I'm going to stay up all night watching horror movies."

Gram's eyes focused. "No you're not."

"Just kidding."

"Then we're even. I was only kidding about the brownie."

Phew. I was relieved that she had come back. It was scary to think that she could be here and so far away at the same time.

"What is this about the mall?" she asked.

86

"Megan O'Connor invited me for a sleepover," I explained.

"That sounds like fun." She looked at me quizzically. "Are you sure you can go a whole twenty-four hours without de-pinking her?"

Gram knows all about Megan and me.

"I can try. Only I have to get her a present."

"When's the party?" Gram asked.

"Uh, tomorrow."

Gram gave me a raised-eyebrow whammy. "Why didn't you tell me before?"

I explained about the mix-up with the invitation.

"Decide what you want to get before we go," she instructed. "I don't want to spend all day there."

"Believe me, I don't either!"

After dinner, I logged into e-mail and found another weird message from Griffin.

**Why don't parents understand that kids' problems are real? They tell me to ignore it when someone calls me "shrimp" or "midget." Like it doesn't matter. If I hear "short stuff" one more time I'm going to flip. And the way kids laugh about it when it is so not funny. Kids I thought were my friends.**

He was still really focused on this height thing. I wrote back, trying to get some more info so I'd feel better equipped to respond. I didn't want to put my foot in my mouth with Griffin.

**Did something unusual happen? I promise I'm taking this seriously. I just don't get why this matters so much all of a sudden. Height was never an issue with you.**

I bit my lip. I didn't know for sure how he'd react. This was new territory for me and Griffin.

He wrote back.

**Okay. It's like this. I tried out for basketball and nearly got laughed out of the gym. And that was just for showing up! I got some serious taunts once I got onto the court.**

I could just imagine the scene—and how much it must have humiliated Griffin.

**To: Thebeast**
**From: Wordpainter**
**That totally bites. Here's my POV:**

1. Some kids love to be mean. They thrive on it.

2. You've got bigger brains than any of those mental midgets—and that's what counts.

I know this probably isn't helping, but believe me, it really is true.

TO: Wordpainter
From: Thebeast

My brain knows that some of the time. It's just that now that we're in middle school I'm the youngest all over again. And the smallest. It's a total drag. I wish I would grow already.

I sent him one last message:

You *will* grow. It's just a fact. Hang in there.

I changed into my pjs and went to brush my teeth. I did an extra good job because my mind was filled with so many things I forgot to stop brushing. I was worried about Griffin. Could he turn into one of those boys Megan had told us about? So bummed by being short that they resort to taking dangerous hormones to grow?

I also had to get onto the Angelina mystery. Signs pointed to the Perkins Day School girl. But I knew enough about investigative reporting to know that just because she looked guilty, that didn't mean she was.

I spit and rinsed and then climbed into bed. I flicked off my lamp. I stared into the dark, thinking about the biggest problem of all.

Megan's present.

I meant to get up early the next morning. I really did. But somehow it didn't happen. Then Gram and I had some quality Saturday morning cartoons and Oat Crunchies time.

Gram confessed to feeling she'd been neglecting me, since all week she'd been searching for her missing adjectives, nouns and all-important verbs behind her study door. To tell the truth, I'd felt her absence.

By the time we were ready to face the world, I had to get to cheerleader practice.

Well, there should be plenty of time to get Megan's present after cheerleading, I told myself. The invitation said the party would start at six.

It was warm out again, so I wasn't surprised to see the cheerleaders practicing outside.

I hurried to the field and scanned the stands. There were fewer people watching today. I was surprised Mrs. Carmichael wasn't here. I thought she'd have hired a bodyguard for Angelina by now.

That girl from Perkins Day School was back. Notebook perched on her knees, she studied every single move, cheer and pointer shouted out by Coach Seltzer. Each time Angelina did something particularly impressive, the girl scribbled furiously.

No doubt about it. The chick was a spy.

# Girl Reporter Run-Run-Runs for Her Story!

I HAD TO question her, and I had to do it without her getting suspicious. I wandered around the stands, heading her way. I tried to make it look as if I was trying to find a better spot to view the practice from.

I arrived at her bleacher. "Hi," I said. "You have a good view here. Mind if I sit with you?"

The girl eyed me up and down. She slammed her notebook shut. "Whatever," she said.

"I'm Casey Smith," I told her.

"Rashidah Jackson." She went back to studying the field.

I tried to think of a way to get her to open up. "I thought it was awesome the way you stood up to Mrs. Carmichael yesterday," I told her. People like compliments.

"She is one piece of work, that lady," Rashidah commented.

"She scares me. You were brave."

"I've seen her type," Rashidah commented, rolling her eyes. "Some of the girls on my team have moms like that."

"So you're a cheerleader?" I asked.

Rashidah glanced at me as if she was trying to figure out what I was up to. "Yeah," she replied warily.

"Do you think this team is any good?"

That's the other thing people like—to tell their opinions.

Rashidah shrugged.

"Is your school competing in the next cheerleaders' meet?" I asked. If they weren't, that would cut Rashidah out of the running as primo suspect.

"Yes . . ." Now she was beginning to sound guarded.

I thought of something—if they were competing, why wasn't Rashidah at her own practice? She'd been here most days—and now even on Saturday. "Why aren't you at your own practice?"

That made her gaskets blow. She stood up. "None of your business, nosy." She grabbed her stuff and stomped away.

Interesting. Though I wasn't sure what any of it meant.

The cheerleaders were doing warm-ups. Well, if you can't sit them down for an interview, join them on the field.

Pad in hand, I jogged over to Ringo. He and the rah-rahs were running around the field.

"Listen, Ringo." I tried to keep my voice low so the rest of the squad wouldn't hear me. "Do the other cheerleaders like Angelina?"

"Sure," Ringo said.

He was hard to keep up with. I had to take, like, three steps for each one of his. Did that mean I was running three times farther?

"Is Angelina really the best one, as you keep saying?" I panted a little as I asked the question.

"Yeah, even the coach thinks so." Ringo wasn't even winded. "She gives Angelina lead positions and stuff."

"Do the other cheerleaders . . ." (pant pant pant) ". . . resent that?"

Ringo looked surprised. "Why would they? We're a team. We pull together. What's good for one is good for all."

I was impressed by his stamina, but not with his idea of reality.

"Get real, Ringo. If you want to help your pal Angelina, you'll need to take off those rose-lensed glasses."

"I don't wear glasses. Not even contacts."

Trying to explain, breathe and jog was more than I could handle. "We'll talk more later." I slowed to a walk and parked myself on a bench. On the field, Ringo sprinted up to Angelina, and fell in step beside her.

I pulled out my notebook and turned to a clean page. I needed to organize what I knew so far:

Angelina is the target of a seriously
nasty prankster.
Incidents so far:
Ankle (could be accident)
Missing cheer book
Eggs in shoes
Bloody Barbie doll effigy (definitely
sicko)

I studied the list. What did they all have in common?

Three of them kept her from being able
to practice.

I bit my pencil. The Barbie doll prank was obviously done to freak her out. But so far, the culprit hadn't actually stated what she wanted. Was she just being super mean to Angelina, or was she trying to keep her out of the competition? Until I knew the answer to that, I wouldn't know the motive. That would make it hard to narrow down the suspects.

And who were those suspects? I bit my lip. Who had something to gain if Angelina dropped out?

### Rashidah

She had an obvious motive, especially if Angelina was as good as Ringo said.

### Could Rashidah have had access to Angelina's locker?

That didn't seem very likely. Rashidah might have no problem getting onto school property, but she'd have a harder time getting into the girls' locker room unnoticed. She'd have an even harder time getting into Angelina's locker.

Angelina did have a habit of leaving things lying around, I realized. And it wasn't too bright of her not to change her lock after things started happening.

It would be hard, but not impossible. Rashidah could have found the locker combination in Angelina's notebook while Angelina was out on the field. She could even have swiped the notebook during practice, broken into the locker and then replaced the notebook once she'd done her prank.

But wait—the Barbie doll. That must have happened sometime during the school day—or just at the start. Would Rashidah have had enough time to get in, get out and get to her own school?

Of course, cutting classes wasn't exactly unheard of.

She was a definite suspect.

As I eyed the cheerleaders, I took down some notes:

Marcy:

She's bossy on the field. She's behind the diet insanity. A true control freak. She's a seventh grader. Likely to be mad if a lowly sixth grader was usurping her spot at the top. (Literally. Marcy

used to top the pyramid! Now it's
Angelina's spot.)

The rest of the cheerleaders: one big
mass of pep. Can't keep them all
straight. There are a whopping twelve
of them! Perky by the dozen.

I looked down at my watch. Boingo! I had to get to the mall pronto!

I didn't even stop to talk to Angelina or Ringo. I just raced to the mall. I had decided to let Gram off the hook since I hadn't been sure what time I'd head over there.

I leaped out of the way as a bunch of high school kids charged out of the entrance. I stepped through the automatic doors and into a hectic swirl of chaos.

Drippy music blasted out of hidden speakers. I wondered if there were secret messages hidden under the soothing sounds, like "Spend money . . . Buy more . . . Go to the food court."

I didn't know where to begin. I knew the big department store, where we bought the basics. It was so large, though, I was afraid I'd need to send up flares in order to find my way out again.

I sighed. The only way out of this ordeal was to enter the heart of the jungle—the mall.

"Try LipSmackers?" A perky girl popped in front of me with a tray full of little goop pots.

"Do you eat them?"

She giggled. "Of course not. It's flavored lip gloss."

"No thanks."

The lights glinted off the shiny surfaces, nearly blinding me. By the time I passed the pretzel vendor for the third time, I wished I'd brought a compass. And that smell . . .

"Agh!" I shrieked as something stung my eye. Something smelly.

"Oh, I'm so sorry," a woman in a red dress said. "I didn't see you there."

She had been spritzing a free sample on a large woman in a green jogging suit. Ms. Jogging Suit held the inside of her wrist up to her nose and sniffed. "Lovely," she declared.

Smelling a sale, the woman with the samples instantly forgot she'd done me damage. All smiles, she held out a box to Ms. Jogger. "Would you like me to gift-wrap it?"

"Oh, no, I was just curious." The jogger wandered away.

The saleswoman caught my eye. "I'm not interested, either," I told her. "And now I'm going to smell like Ecstatic Dreams all day."

Focus, Casey, I ordered myself. You're running out of time. I bopped into Face-2-Face.

"Wouldn't you just love a free makeover?" an overdone girl crooned at me.

I gaped at her. Why would she think I needed a makeover? Did she think there was something wrong with me?

I noticed women and girls scoping themselves out in the millions of mirrors that surrounded us. Half the time they'd look and cringe. Then they'd wander over to the makeup counters.

Was that the plan all along? The reason for all the mirrors and harsh lighting? I shuddered, then pressed on.

I had made it in and out of every single store on the floor. I'd gotten lost four times, and almost ended up getting spritzed again by the perfume perpetrator.

Shopping is exhausting.

I ducked into Tweens. I had heard Megan and Toni mention it.

It was nice and small compared to the vast expanse of some of the other stores. Even better, there were no makeup counters or lethal perfume spritzers.

I flipped through a rack of tops. I saw plenty of

things I thought Melody would like, but nothing for Megan.

I was heading for another rack when I heard a familiar voice: Mrs. Carmichael.

"If you would stick to a diet it would be easier to find clothes that fit," Mrs. Carmichael complained.

"Mom, can we just do this?" Lauren grumbled.

"Honestly, I don't understand," Mrs. Carmichael said. "You have such a pretty face. If only you tried a little harder—"

"Mom, please!" Lauren sounded really unhappy.

"Look at Angelina. She excels in everything she does. She keeps up her grades and she's a talented cheerleader."

"Are you ever going to quit going on about that stupid squad?" Now Lauren sounded irritated.

"Stupid squad? Did you say 'stupid squad'?" Mrs. Carmichael's voice dripped ice. "I'll have you know that my time as cheerleader was the happiest time of my life."

"I didn't make it, okay?" Lauren yelled. "It didn't end my life. In fact, I never wanted to be on that stupid squad in the first place. I only tried out because you made me."

"Is it so terrible that I want both my daughters to enjoy the same experiences I did?"

"Didn't you even care that there was no way I'd be good at it?" Lauren retorted. "Or that I didn't *want* to get good at it?"

"Angelina—"

Lauren cut her off. "Quit throwing Angelina in my face. She's the perfect daughter and I'm the disappointment. That message has come through loud and clear."

"Stop being so dramatic."

So Lauren had tried out for the squad and didn't make it. The way Mrs. Carmichael treated Angelina and Lauren so differently must be causing a whopping case of sibling rivalry.

Uh-oh. Any minute now they would find me on the other side of this pillar. I didn't want them to think I was eavesdropping—especially since I was.

I tipped down my chin so that my hair fell into my face. Going without a trim for as long as I have can certainly come in handy. Instant disguise. Keeping my face down, I wove around the clothing racks and out of the store.

The front of the store was all glass, so I kept my head down as I walked away. I spotted black high-tops facing me.

I moved to the left. So did the black high-tops.

I moved to the right. So did the black high-tops.

I stood still. So did the black high-tops.

"Can I have this dance?" a teasing voice said.

I looked up—right into Tyler McKenzie's warm brown eyes.

"Cha cha cha," I said.

"All that dancing made me thirsty," he said. "Wanna go grab a soda or something?"

Did I? "You bet."

As we headed for Hole in the Mall, I snuck peeks at Tyler. Did he worry about his height, like Griffin? Or how he looked, like the boys Toni talked about?

Nah. He was just too perfect.

We slid into a booth. I realized I was starving, so Tyler and I split an order of fries along with our Slurpees. A few tables over, a group started singing "Happy Birthday."

"Oh, no!" I said. The singing triggered my panic button.

"What's wrong?" Tyler asked. "Did a fry go down the wrong way?"

I explained about Megan's party and that I couldn't think of a good present.

"Hm. That's a tough one."

"I just don't think I can wrap my mind around all that pinkness," I complained.

Tyler munched thoughtfully on a french fry. Then his eyes lit up. "Got it. How about a book?"

"A book," I repeated. "Possible. What book?"

We ate a few more fries while we thought. "I know," Tyler said. "You liked *Little Women*. What about Megan?"

My mouth dropped open. It was a perfect choice. There was enough stuff about clothes and boys and romance to keep Megan interested. What I liked best, though, was the main character, Jo March. She was a writer with her feet on the ground. Awesome kid.

"You are a total genius," I told Tyler.

He beamed. "I try."

Maybe the mall wasn't such a bad place after all.

# Picky Eaters Go for the Dough!

"CASEY!" MEGAN GREETED me at her front door. "I was afraid you changed your mind about coming."

I stepped into the front hall. "Sorry I'm late. Time just got away from me."

By the time I had made it home from the mall, it was practically time to leave. I would have opted for the store's gift-wrapping service, but the line was too long.

You'd think a rectangle wouldn't be so hard to wrap.

I hoped Megan wouldn't mind that I'd used Christmas wrapping. Hey, it was festive, and there weren't little Santas on it. It was hollies. That could be for a birthday. Of course, it would have worked better if Megan's name was Holly.

I held out the present.

Megan's eyes widened. "Th-thanks."

I could hear high-pitched squeals from the living room. I braced myself. "So who else is here?" I asked.

"Come on in and say hi to everyone." Her voice was unnaturally chirpy, even for her. It occurred to me she had hostess nerves.

I followed Megan into the living room.

Samantha, Marcy and Angelina sat together on the couch. I was surprised to see the cheerleaders here, especially since Samantha and Marcy were seventh graders. Then I remembered: Samantha and Marcy were on the yearbook with Megan. And Angelina had one or two classes with Megan.

Toni and Melody sat on the floor beside the coffee table. So there were three of us and four of the perky patrol. We were outnumbered. This could be a loooooooong night.

Megan placed my present on the pile of loot.

Mrs. O'Connor came in. "Is everyone here now?"

"Yup." Megan faced us all. "We're going to make our own pizzas," she announced. "Doesn't that sound like fun?"

"Pizza?" Marcy said. "That's so fattening."

Megan's smile faltered. She blinked really hard. Her party had just started and already there was a hitch.

"We have all sorts of healthy toppings," Mrs. O'Connor assured Marcy.

Darn. Did that mean I wouldn't be able to make a double-cheese, sausage and pepperoni pizza?

We filed into the kitchen. A long counter held a row of plates and bowls and little jars filled with toppings and spices. They had really gone all out.

We sat on stools along the counter. "Maybe we should just eat the mushrooms," Marcy suggested, eyeing the spread.

"Sorry, girls." Mrs. O'Connor plopped a round of unbaked dough in front of each of us. "My house, my rules. You have to eat an actual dinner."

"Well, if we have to," Samantha said.

We went to work. I noticed Marcy and Samantha piled up their pizzas like the rest of us.

"I never knew cooking could be cool," Toni said. She dumped loads of garlic onto her dough. "Finally, I'll get enough garlic."

"Good thing there aren't any boys here," Marcy teased. "You're going to have killer bad breath."

"You all better be nice to me," Toni warned. "Or I'll breathe on you all night."

"In that case, I'm adding more garlic." I

grabbed the bowl of garlic from her. "In self-defense."

"What are you making?" Angelina asked Melody.

"I thought I'd go exotic," Melody replied. She dripped peanut sauce onto the dough. Then she added peppers, onions and chicken. If you didn't know it was supposed to be pizza, it would be good.

A plain round of dough sat in front of Angelina. Melody held out the peanut sauce to her. "Want some?" Melody asked.

"Oh, no," Angelina said. "I can't. I'm allergic to peanuts."

"So is my sister," Marcy commented. "Do you get all blotchy?"

"Worse," Angelina said. "My throat closes up. Once I almost died. That's how we found out about it. When I was little, I took a bite of my sister's sandwich and wham—bye-bye me."

"Your mom warned me about your allergy, Angelina," Mrs. O'Connor said. "Don't worry. There aren't any nuts in the birthday cake. It's white cake with strawberries."

It figured that Megan would have a vanilla cake. She's a vanilla kind of girl.

While the pizzas baked we talked about what we liked and hated about middle school. We actually had more in common than I'd imagined. The rah-rahs were sort of helium-headed, but they were friendly. They even seemed interested in *Real News*—they all complimented Toni on her photos. They'd seen them and admired them in each issue.

Hard to believe they were actually paying attention.

When the pizzas were ready, we all traded bites. Angelina's three-cheese with garlic was so delicious we all tried some. I realized we hadn't left much for her.

I held mine out to her. I had loaded it up so much that I almost couldn't fit it into my mouth. "Take some."

"No thanks," she said. "I have plenty." She took a teeny nibble of the corner of what was left of her pizza.

I also noticed that when she got up to get more water, she slid some of the pizza into a napkin and threw it out.

This was weird behavior. So odd that I didn't even ask about it.

After the pizza it was time for presents and cake. Megan gushed after each one.

Megan's eyes widened when she unwrapped my gift. "*Little Women.*" She held the book up for everyone to see.

"You're going to love it, honey," her mom said.

"Oh, Casey, thank you," Megan said.

She sounded like she really meant it. And there was that hundred-watt glow in her face. I owed Tyler big time.

When we were done eating, we went up to Megan's room. Marcy flopped down on the bed. "I ate too much," she complained.

"What do you want to do now?" Megan asked. "I have videos, some games. . . ."

Marcy rolled over and sat up. "I know! Let's do makeovers."

There was that word again. "Not for me," I said. "I like me the way I am."

"Angelina, you have the best hair," Marcy said. "Let's make hairstyles."

Angelina sat at Megan's ruffled dressing table. "I like Toni's hair," she protested.

Tonight Toni had her curls pulled away from her face with about ten little glitter clips.

"No one messes with my hair," Toni declared.

Megan went into the bathroom and came back out with a basket of hair accessories. "I'll see if my mom will let us use her makeup." She left and came back in with an armload of magazines and a bagful of makeup.

"Great!" Samantha said. She grabbed the magazines. "We can get ideas from these."

Marcy, Samantha and Megan pored over those

pages as if they held the answer to some huge secret of the universe.

"She looks like you," Samantha said. She held the magazine out to Megan.

"You think so?" Megan tucked her blond hair behind her ear as she bent over the magazine picture. "You really think I look like that? Thanks."

"I think this one looks kind of like me," Marcy said.

I noticed Melody, Toni and I had wound up on the floor on the other side of the room.

The Thems and the Us's. Was that because the Thems looked like the girls in the magazines and we didn't? Or because the Thems were the ones who cared?

"Ooh," Megan cooed. "Here's an article on 'N Sync. I think Lance is so cute. Don't you?"

"Don't ask Angelina," Marcy teased. "She already has a boyfriend."

"Stop." Angelina giggled. "I do not."

"I wish I looked like her." Samantha held up a picture.

"Why would you want to look like that?" Toni asked. "She looks half dead."

Samantha laughed. "Oh, she does not."

"Who's up for a makeover?" Marcy asked. "Melody, want to try some different makeup ideas?" I couldn't tell if Marcy was being mean or being sincere.

"No thank you," Melody said quietly. She seemed bummed.

"Melody looks good the way she is," I said. "Why should we try to look like the girls in the magazines?" I stood and paced. "All of this focus on looks and diets. It makes me want to throw up."

"That's how a lot of models stay so slim," Marcy said with a laugh.

"That is so gross," Toni commented. "I hate puking."

"Maybe so," Marcy said. "But it works."

Samantha giggled. "We should try it. We stuffed ourselves like little piggies tonight."

"What do you think?" Marcy asked. "Are we all in?"

I gaped at them.

Were they nuts?

# Danger—Entering the Barf Zone!

THE ROOM WAS totally silent. Why didn't somebody say something? Why didn't *I* say something?

I guess I was stunned. Puking as a party game? Sick or what?

We all sat there, staring at each other.

Then Toni snorted. "Get real. That is so whacked. I am so not doing it."

"Me either," Melody and I chimed in together.

"You know throwing up is part of a real eating disorder," Megan said. "It's called bulimia. It can make you really, really sick. There's something called anorexia, too."

"That's the one where you don't eat, right?" Samantha asked. She giggled. "I wish I could catch that!"

"No you don't," Megan warned. "It's a serious

illness. You can die from it."

"You know, models don't even look like that." Toni grabbed a magazine. "See this one here?" She folded back the pages and held out a picture. "This has been airbrushed. They took out part of her leg to make it look thinner."

"No way," Marcy protested.

"Yes, way," Toni replied. "You can light people so that they look thin. If you stand a certain way, you look thinner. They airbrush their faces so they never have pimples or lines. They whiten teeth. Make boobs bigger or smaller, depending on what they want."

I was impressed. Toni seemed to know what she was talking about.

"People make loads of money turning these girls into totally different people," Toni said, tossing her curls. "So even these models don't look like these models. It's all a big fat lie. Heck, with digital, soon they won't need any real girls at all."

Megan flipped through a magazine. "These images are pretty unrealistic," she said. "It's part of the whole body-image problem."

She waved the magazine at us. "Did you know that about fifty percent of girls our age have already dieted because they think they're too fat, and only about ten percent of them actually are?"

"So why do they think they have to diet?" Melody asked.

"Pictures like these," Toni said. "The media tells them people are supposed to look this way."

"But we can get decent fashion ideas from those magazines," Marcy protested. She had started playing with Angelina's hair while Samantha applied makeup.

"It's a fact," Toni complained. "Girls are judged by their appearance more than boys are."

"Exactly," Melody agreed. "If you want to insult a girl you say she's ugly or fat. If you want to insult a boy you call him dumb or weak."

"Or short," I added, thinking of Griffin.

"What's the big deal?" Marcy asked. "Face it. To be accepted and popular and successful, you have to look good. That's just reality."

"Maybe so," Megan conceded. "But is it a reality we want to live with?"

"My sister, Lauren, feels bad about how she looks," Angelina said. I realized she'd been pretty silent on the subject up until now. "And my mom just makes it worse."

*That* I could believe.

"I think if my mom quit picking on her, she'd do better," she added.

"Well, you have nothing to worry about," Marcy said. "You're so pretty and skinny already."

I felt weird about that skinny part. That shouldn't be what Angelina was rewarded for.

"Let's finish your makeover," Samantha said. "Then Ringo won't be able to resist you."

"Megan," Melody said, her voice faint. "I . . . I'm not feeling very well. Would you mind terribly if I called my mum to pick me up?"

A look of concern crossed Megan's face. "Do you think it was your east-west pizza?"

"I . . . I think it's the flu."

"I hope it isn't contagious," Marcy muttered.

Not unless liking a boy who likes a different girl is contagious, I thought.

While Melody called her mom, I considered leaving with Melody—as a show of solidarity, and also because once she left it would leave me and Toni to fight off the fluff factor. Then I looked at Megan. Another defection would freak her out. Driving off her guests would make her lose out on the Perfect Hostess award.

"Feel better," Megan called after Melody as she left with her mom a few minutes later.

"Okay, who's next?" Marcy asked, lip gloss wand in hand.

Toni and I backed away.

"I know," Megan suggested. "Let's play Twister!"

Interesting. Marcy and Samantha both seemed

perfectly willing to give up the diets and the makeovers when they were offered something else—something fun—to do. I wondered if all this diet and makeup junk was just a pose to make them feel more grown-up.

I had a feeling, though, that Angelina was another story.

The next morning I found Angelina alone in Megan's living room. She sat reading an encyclopedia.

"Doing homework?" I asked.

"This is an old encyclopedia," she told me. "You know how I know?" She held it out to me. It was open to a page about dinosaurs. "They don't call it brontosaurus anymore. It's been renamed apatosaurus."

"Oh." Big whoop. "What's with you and dinosaurs?" I asked.

Angelina shrugged. "I don't know. I like how they look. And how they're so big and powerful. It's cool to think that they were here millions of years ago. It makes me wonder about how things were back then."

She sighed. "There's so much to learn about them. There are new discoveries all the time."

I didn't know how long we would be alone, so

I cut to the chase. "Who do you consider your main cheerleading rival?"

She looked startled by the change of topic. "That girl from the other school, I guess."

"What about someone on the Trumbull team? Someone who would have easier access to your locker."

Angelina looked puzzled. "Why would someone on the squad want me to quit? I can't imagine any of the girls being that mean."

She had the same rosy view as Ringo. Was I such a terrible person that I could see that all was not so sunny?

"You're new to the squad," I suggested. "Have any of the older girls been bummed that you get so many of the important stunts to do?"

"I don't think so."

"What about Marcy?" I pressed.

"What about Marcy?" Marcy asked as she came into the room.

"Not Marcy," I said. "Marthy. Marthy Stewart. Angelina suggested I get pointers from Martha Stewart for present-wrapping."

Marcy looked at me as if she felt sorry for me. At that moment, I felt sorry for me, too.

Luckily Megan came into the room. "Are you going to see Melody soon?" she asked. "She left her bracelet at my house." She held it out to me.

It was a copper bracelet. Exactly like the one I saw in the locker room the day we found the blood-covered Barbie in Angelina's gym locker.

My heart thumped. Was *Melody* the perp?

# Goth Gal Goes Goofy!

MY BRAIN FELT like it had been through a blender. It felt oozy and gooey up there under my hair.

All that talk of image and looks had set my mind spinning in the first place. But twirling it around in the other direction was the Angelina mystery.

Could Melody be behind the pranks? I didn't want it to be true. But it was possible.

Weirdly enough, I liked Angelina. That was already a major mind melt. Me, liking an elf cheerleader.

"Hey, Casey," Gram greeted me from the living room when I got back home. "Have fun?"

"Fun isn't exactly what I'd call it." I plopped into the chair opposite her.

I thought she must be back on her game. She

was wearing her red kimono over a green T-shirt and purple leggings. That's more her style when she's burning up the computer keys.

"You didn't have a good time?" she asked. "I'm sorry. Did something happen?"

"No, it's more like the whole vibe was on the strange side."

I told Gram about what we had talked about—minus the suggestion to puke as a party game.

Gram sighed. "This is a big issue—at all ages," she said. "The emphasis on physical beauty in this culture can have a devastating effect on anyone—not to mention girls your age."

"Toni told us that most of those pictures are retouched. Is that true?"

Gram nodded. "Some more than others, obviously, but yes."

"Megan says that eating disorders are starting younger and younger," I said.

"Sad to say, they're on the rise," Gram said. "So many things are starting younger."

I kept wishing Gram would contradict what I was saying, but all she was doing was confirming.

"All this focus on looks," I grumbled. "First they make it matter too much and then they make it too hard to live up to."

"Who's they?" Gram asked gently.

"I don't know," I responded glumly. I like it

better when I can identify the enemy. But who could I pin this on? "The media?" I said hopefully. I needed a target.

"Well, the media contributes to the problem, yes. But it is never just one thing that creates an eating disorder."

I kicked the table leg. "Well, whoever they are, I'm really mad at them."

"You have every right to be," Gram said. "And I hope you will do all you can to fight them at every turn."

"How can I do that? I don't know who they are, remember?"

"Well, by writing about it, for one thing. That's your strength, Casey. It's a powerful tool. The more you expose this issue, force people to examine it, the more common sense is likely to prevail."

"Maybe," I said. "I want concrete action."

"Take them on head-on. If you're bothered by those unrealistic images and articles in the magazines you read, write to the publishers."

"I don't read those magazines," I protested. Geez. I thought she knew me better than that.

She smiled. "Fine. Start a boycott of the products you think are the worst offenders. But on the personal level, take a cue from your friend Toni. Recognize when you're being manipulated and laugh it off. It's ridiculous. The idea that a Barbie doll represents ideal womanhood is absurd. If she were a real woman with those proportions she wouldn't actually be able to stand up."

"Really?"

"Also, you know the old chestnut, 'Beauty is in the eye of the beholder'?"

"Of course." Usually Gram doesn't lay the clichés on me.

"Well, it's also in the eye of the particular moment in history in a particular culture."

"Huh?" I said. "You lost me."

"The concept of beauty has changed throughout the ages," Gram explained. "Look at art and advertising from previous centuries and decades. At a time when food was hard to come by, heavier women were considered beautiful—it showed they had enough to eat."

"So how come that changed? Why is everybody supposed to be skinny now?"

"Well, there are a few answers to that question. First of all, that's not true in other countries. Or even in this one."

She had lost me again. She could tell.

"In the African-American community, eating disorders are much more rare," she explained. "Studies have been done that show that young black women tend to score much higher on self-esteem and body issues than young white women."

"Why?" I asked.

Gram sighed. "It's the one time racism may actually have had a surprising benefit. Because it has taken so long for black models to be used in the magazines, young black girls haven't been comparing themselves to these unrealistic images."

I flashed on Rashidah. She was certainly heavier than any of the cheerleaders at Trumbull, but she carried herself with a lot more confidence than they did. Angelina looked like most of those girls in the magazines, yet she seemed more unsure of herself. Melody, too. She was worried about her relationship with Ringo. And instead of thinking that maybe Ringo liked Angelina because they were both cheerleaders, Melody thought it was because of how they compared in looks. She turned it into a body image problem.

"There are those who feel the emphasis on very young, thin girls in the last decade is actually political," Gram went on. "Throughout history, there have been cultural backlashes against the progress women have made. So, now that women can work with men, earn like men, have far more access to positions of power than they ever used to, they are confronted by images that tell them that none of that actually matters. They will only be valued if they are actually weak, small, childlike and helpless."

I could tell Gram was on a roll. I figured I'd let her rip.

"Despite how much more powerful we've become," Gram went on, "the culture creates dissatisfaction about themselves in many women."

"This has happened before?" I asked.

"As women fought to get the vote, their corsets became tighter and tighter. So as women gained more freedom, they were reined in by fashion, subjected to greater restriction in their clothing."

"It's starting to affect boys, too," I commented. "I can't decide if I'm glad that now they have the same junk to deal with that girls do. Or if that makes it seem even worse and harder to fight. The problem is spreading."

Gram took my face in her hands. "Somehow I think you'll help fight the infection."

I didn't feel so sure. But I was glad for her vote of confidence. It made me feel ready to write. Ready to take 'em all on. Megan had a good idea. This was an important story.

The phone rang. I went to answer it.

"Hallo, Casey." I recognized Melody's accent immediately. "How was the party after I left?"

"Weird. It would have been more fun if you had stayed."

"I couldn't stand a single minute more. Those cheerleaders! What twits! And that Angelina. Who does she think she is?"

The famous British reserve was nowhere in evidence. "Uh, I don't know. . . ." I didn't know what else to say.

"How can Ringo like her? She's such a . . . a . . . nit!"

I wondered if that was different from a twit.

"I couldn't believe she tried to get Ringo to do a partners' routine with her. The nerve."

"Uh, Melody, that was Ringo's idea," I pointed out.

"Are you sticking up for her?" Melody demanded.

"No, of course not," I said quickly.

"Well, I wish she would just quit the squad. Then Ringo wouldn't spend all that time with her."

She hung up on me. I stared at the phone.

Judging from that conversation, I had to admit Melody was my most likely suspect.

Oh rats. This investigation had just taken an unhappy turn.

# Facts on Figures Reveal Image Insanity!

MONDAY MORNING I went to the *Real News* office first thing. I had done a decent amount of research on the body-image story, and I wanted to enter the statistics into the computer. I wasn't sure yet what the angle would be, but I knew I would figure it out once I got a sense of the stats.

The facts were scary:

Models are now taller and thinner than they ever used to be. In the 1950s the average model was 5 feet, 8 inches, and 132 pounds, which was still taller and thinner than the average American woman. Now the average model is an astonishing 5 feet, 10 inches, and 110 pounds. That's twenty-five percent lighter than most American women. Only four percent of all American women have this body naturally. Which means ninety-six percent are getting the message that they don't look like the ideal.

The diet industry makes big profits from an obsession with thinness—and the likelihood of failure. One major weight-loss program reported $85 million in profits last year. Ninety percent of all diets fail. Do the math.

At the same time, the country is getting fatter. Obesity is at an all-time high, and it's fueled partly by all this dieting—which seems ironic, but it actually has a medical basis. Yo-yo dieting does something screwy to the metabolism, and often people gain more weight when they break a diet than they wanted to lose in the first place.

The other culprit? Some say the couch-potato lifestyle. Too much TV, video-game playing and computer surfing leads to a less active lifestyle. Junk food rules. It's everywhere. And busy people find it more convenient to rely on fast food than to make a low-fat, healthy meal three times a day.

What seems to be missing in this mix is good old common sense. That's what Gram and I had talked about this morning. The idea should be: Feel good, be healthy, and you'll automatically look good. Instead, though, it's all backward.

After all the research I had done last night and this morning, I started thinking I was right about Angelina. I was pretty sure she was one of those starving girls. She displayed all the signs of anorexia.

"Casey, I'm glad you're here," Angelina said as she burst into the newsroom. Ringo followed behind her.

"I told you she'd be easy to find," Ringo said.

Angelina thrust a piece of paper at me. "I found this in my locker."

I glanced at the typewritten note.

```
Quit the squad—if you know what's
good for you!!!
```

I freaked. Those were almost Melody's exact words last night.

I studied the note. It was printed on plain old paper. Nothing special about the paper—or the font.

If only printed words had accents! That would be the tip-off. None of these words had a particularly British slant. While it didn't prove Melody didn't do it, it didn't disprove it either.

Wait a sec. "This was in your gym locker?" I asked. "With your brand-new lock?"

Angelina nodded miserably as she sat at Dalmatian Station. "You know, nothing is worth this feeling. I think I should just do what they want and quit the squad. At least for now," she added quickly.

Ringo knelt by her. "But you love to cheer, don't you?"

Angelina looked down at her hands. "Well . . . yes . . ."

"We'll solve this," I promised. "And we'll solve it fast enough to keep you in the meet."

As they left, I thought that I had just made a promise I might not be able to keep. But I had to try.

Pesky classes got in the way of any more detecting. I managed some mull time, but no new investigation.

The Frosted Cheerios did seem to get along. I didn't get the sense that Marcy and Samantha were such good actresses that they could pretend they were Angelina's friends one minute and then torture her the next. They were dingdongs, but they didn't strike me as two-faced.

The perp had finally stated what she was truly after. If Angelina didn't quit, what would happen next?

So far, none of the pranks had put Angelina in any real danger.

I wondered if it would stay that way.

# Who, What, Where, When and Huh?

I SPENT THE morning thinking about who. I spent the afternoon thinking about how. I was so muddled I gave the wrong answers in Spanish class, and I had even studied.

Did we have a junior safecracker at Trumbull? Now *that* would be a story! Maybe I should dust the locker for fingerprints. Only I wasn't sure what to do about the prints after I collected them. Somehow I didn't think the administration kept our fingerprints on file. At least not yet . . .

I headed for the *Real News* office for our Monday afternoon story meeting. Everyone else was already there. Ringo stood in the corner touching his toes and stretching. Gary and Megan were going over some notes. Toni had a bunch of magazines spread out in front of her.

I checked out the covers. They were all fashion magazines, like the ones from Megan's sleepover.

"Scouting for a new look?" I asked.

"Not a chance," Toni replied. "It's for a story."

Megan looked up from her notes. "You have a story to pitch? Great!"

Toni tipped back in her chair. "Photo-essay. To go along with the body-image theme." She held out her hands as if she was indicating a banner going across the page. "Before and After: How photos lie!"

"I like it already," Megan said.

I did, too. It was exactly what Gram and I had talked about—fighting back against the media pressure by exposing the unreality of the ideal.

"What I want to do is show how the original pictures are distorted, so I figured I'd shoot befores and afters," Toni explained. "And also mark up existing ads to show how they might have been altered."

"Excellent!" Then Megan frowned. "I'm just having second thoughts about the whole issue being devoted to this one theme. Does it slant the newspaper too much?"

"Yes!" Gary said. "See? Now you're making sense."

"Still, it's important to get the all the facts in,

and that takes up space," Megan said. She tapped her pen on the table.

"How about this," I offered. "Instead of a full-fledged story, I'll do a sidebar to go along with Toni's photo-essay. You know, stats, facts, polls. That kind of thing. That way we get the info out, but save space for other stories."

"That's a great idea," Megan exclaimed. "Let's hold the center spread for Toni's pictures and Casey's sidebar."

Gary narrowed his brown eyes as he scrutinized me. "Casey Smith? Volunteering to give up column inches? What gives?"

"I do have a story," I admitted. "It's an important one. Very front-page news."

"Do you ever have an idea that you don't assume is front-page news?" Gary taunted.

I ignored him. "As you know, the cheerleader meet is coming up, and—"

Gary slammed his hand on the table. "Hold on! That story is mine!"

I folded my arms across my chest. "What exactly is 'that story,' Gar?"

Brown eyes to brown eyes. Finally, he blinked. He stuck out his lower lip. I guess some girls would find his pout cute. Not I. I knew I'd just won.

Then he regrouped. Gary was actually quicker

with his brains than on his feet. He just refused to admit he was only a jock wannabe.

"Any story involving teams or sports is my beat," he protested. He faced Megan. "You've assigned me stories that I didn't want just because they fell into that category."

Okay, so he was right. But that didn't mean I had to agree with him.

"Let's hear what Casey has to say before we make any decisions," Megan said.

Sometimes the fact that she's so pink and prim is a good thing.

"Okay," I said. "There is a dangerous prank puller in this school. The target? Angelina Carmichael."

I spilled all, and Ringo backed me up. Though he wasn't sure that Angelina would want anything printed about her in the newspaper.

"The victim speaks!" I argued. "It would be a great angle. We can talk about how she felt during this ordeal. She'd feel better if she got a chance to vent. I know I would!"

"You vent even if there's nothing to vent about," Gary commented.

"The thing is," I continued, as if I hadn't heard his bogus remark, "I'm guessing it will get worse for Angelina before it gets better. Unless I figure out who the culprit is, and fast."

Megan's face was clouded with concern. "Poor Angelina. I had no idea. That explains why she barely ate at the party."

I had a feeling there was another, far more upsetting reason for Angelina's lack of food consumption. But I wasn't ready to go there. Not in public.

Hey—I could be sensitive, too! Especially when I knew for a fact that I didn't have all the facts— about Angelina *or* about anorexia.

"We should all do everything we can to help," Megan said. She turned to me. "If it's an appropriate story, we'll run it."

Appropriate? Whatever. I knew that once I tracked down the perp I'd find a way to write it up so that there was no way Megan could avoid printing my story.

I shut my notebook and shoved it into my backpack. "I've got an investigation to conduct."

I tore out of the newsroom. Not fast enough to lose Gary, though. He was hot on my trail.

He grabbed my arm and spun me around.

"Hey!" I yanked my arm back.

He was really steamed. "I asked you to cover this story, and you turned me down flat."

"That's because it wasn't *this* story," I pointed out. "You wanted me to cover a dumb athletic event. This is a newsbreaking criminal investigation."

"It's still my beat," he insisted. "And I'll cover it on my own."

I bit my lip. Now that he knew about the incidents, what if he uncovered the culprit before I did? Not because he was a better reporter than I was. It was the Gary cuteness factor that could work in his favor. The cheerleaders would open up to him like a whale sucking in waves.

Man. Looks really did play into success and failure.

Unfair!

Then I had a realization. There were some things that even good looks couldn't help with.

"So, Gary," I said. "Just how do you plan to get to the bottom of this story?"

He rolled his eyes as if I'd asked the stupidest question he'd ever heard. "How do you think? Like any good investigative reporter."

"Gee, Gary . . ." I put a finger on my chin. "Isn't checking out the crime scene an important part of an investigation?"

"Of course it is," Gary snapped. "Look, Casey. Quit acting like you're the only one who knows how to be a good reporter."

"Okay, Gary. Go for it. There's the crime scene."

I pointed at the door to the girls' locker room.

Gary's cheeks flamed.

Hah! Gotcha!

"Fine, Casey," he muttered. "You made your point. Can we at least work on this together?"

The words "Get real" were on the tip of my tongue when Rashidah walked out of the girls' locker room.

My eyes bugged. What was she doing in there? There went my theory that she wouldn't have access.

"Oh, hey, Gary," she greeted the jockaroni beside me. He nodded back at her.

My head whipped back and forth between Gary and Rashidah.

I was really glad no one had snapped my picture. No amount of retouching would de-frogify my face at that moment.

CHAPTER
18

# Coaches Blind to Meanies on Their Squads!

"You know each other?" I asked.

"Yeah," Gary answered. He was obviously surprised by my surprise. "Casey, this is my cousin Rashidah. Rashidah, this is—"

"We've met," Rashidah said, eyeing me warily. She must know that Gary wrote for *Real News*. Was she putting two and two together and adding me up to an investigative reporter?

"How did you get into the girls' locker room?" I demanded.

She raised an eyebrow. "With my feet, how else?" she snapped. "Gary, I'll meet you on the court." She used those feet to take off.

It occurred to me that having Gary in on this story would come in handy.

"What gives?" he asked me. "There was some

strange vibe between you and Rashidah."

"I have reason to believe that your cousin is the one after Angelina."

"No way," Gary exclaimed.

"Up until now, all I had on Rashidah was motive," I said. "She's been spying on the squad to size up the competition, and from the looks of things, Angelina is what really makes the squad shine."

"That doesn't make Rashidah the culprit," he protested. "A lot of teams will be competing."

"Don't you see?" I said. "We just saw Rashidah come out of the girls' locker room. Now I know that she has access, too."

"Not to Angelina's locker combination," Gary argued.

"That part is tough to pin on any of the suspects," I admitted. In fact, that part was making me nuts. But I wasn't going to tell Gary that.

"Rashidah has been here on days that incidents happened," I pointed out.

Gary sighed. "I know that Rashidah has been hanging around Trumbull a lot lately. But it's not what you think. She's got a visitor's pass from the office."

"Ooh, like that explains anything. What's her deal?" I demanded. "Why would anyone hang around Trumbull if they don't have to?"

"Look, Casey," Gary said. "I know you're not going to back off on this. Just let me do the questioning, okay? I can make it sound like conversation, not interrogation."

"And I can't?" My ears burned red with indignation.

"Chill. I'll go talk to Rashidah." He jogged away.

I hurried into the girls' locker room. I wanted to see if Rashidah had done anything to Angelina's locker.

Maybe Gary could get Rashidah's fingerprints. Then I could compare them to the fingerprints from the locker.

Yeah. That would happen. Not.

The whole place was empty. Wasn't there a practice today? I popped my head into the gym. No cheerleaders in sight. Not a rah anywhere.

I stopped by to check the schedule by Coach Seltzer's office. There had been one scheduled. So what happened?

I knocked on Coach Seltzer's door. I had some questions for her, anyway.

"Come in," I heard her answer.

I opened the door and stepped inside. "Hi. I'm Casey Smith. I write for *Real News*."

She swiveled around in her chair. "What can I do for you?"

I glanced around the office. Wow. Pep Central. The walls were covered with pennants and posters. A glass case held trophies. A bulletin board had stop-action photos of amazing stunts. The inches not taken up by girls standing on their heads and leaping over each other were filled with inspirational quotes. The bookcase held videos labeled by date and event.

"Are those from Trumbull teams?" I asked.

"No. From other teams I've coached. And from my own days as a cheerleader."

"I'm writing a story about the upcoming meet, and I had a few questions." I took out my notebook. Maybe I could work my way around to Angelina's perp by starting with the meet.

"Sure."

"Actually, my first question is, why was practice canceled today?"

"On Saturday, I recognized the warning signs of overtraining," Coach Seltzer explained. "The girls can become so driven that they push themselves too far. I wanted to remind them to have fun, to take breaks."

"They had Sunday off," I pointed out. "Wasn't that enough time?"

Coach Seltzer smiled. "A day off has a lot more meaning if it's unexpected. Like playing hooky with permission."

Made sense to me. And it gave me an easy lead straight to topic A. "You say the girls are driven. Do you think that might make them do crazy things? Like those pranks being played on Angelina?"

Coach Seltzer shook her head. "I've seen pranks before, but this is different. Sometimes a team member may be picked on, but it's usually someone who is disliked, or the weakest member. Angelina doesn't fit that profile."

"Could jealousy be the cause?" I asked.

"There is often competition on a squad. But frankly, that hasn't been true here. The squad really does pull together. But I did give them a very stern lecture. I won't tolerate that behavior."

I wondered if she could actually spot a meanie on the squad. Kids are good at hiding things from grown-ups.

"One of the benefits of cheerleading," the coach continued, "as with any sport, is the teamwork and cooperation. It also helps to develop a strong sense of confidence and good healthy relationship to the body."

"But all this emphasis on looks," I argued. "Doesn't that do the exact opposite?"

"Eating disorders can be a problem among cheerleaders," she admitted. "In fact, a large percentage of them struggle with weight issues. It's important that they have a sensible attitude toward weight."

"How do you keep them sensible?" I asked. Most of what I'd seen them do was totally bonkers.

"I give out pamphlets on good nutrition and emphasize how important it is in order to do their best," she replied. "Cheerleading is an extremely strenuous sport—fad diets are a no-no."

Well, I just got a good clue that Coach Seltzer didn't know as much about her squad as she thought. She had obviously never witnessed the cabbage soup lunch menu.

"We do weigh the girls—making sure they keep to a minimum weight," she added.

"What about maximum weight?" I thought back to the girl who had been booted off the squad.

"It may sound cruel, but the girls are expected to keep to a maximum weight as well," the coach replied. "For me, that's a matter of good health."

"What would you do if you thought a girl had an eating disorder?" I asked.

"I would try to get her to talk to me, and let her know that it could get her off the squad. It is just too risky. She could do herself serious—and permanent—damage." She shook her head. "I hope it doesn't get to that point. The girls are really looking forward to the meet."

"Are you saying you have girls with eating disorders on the squad now?" I asked.

She gave me a look. She must have realized it was too late to take back that little slip now. "Off the record only," she said.

I nodded.

"I have suspicions about one or two of the girls, yes."

I had a feeling Angelina was on the top of that list. Which meant Angelina might not be able to perform if she continued her weird dieting. And the culprit would get exactly what she wanted.

I wondered if Angelina knew that.

# CHAPTER 19

# Girl Reporter Corners Pit Bull!

I DECIDED TO go over to Angelina's. She needed to know that she was already in danger of being off the squad—with or without the help of the perp. I was pretty convinced she had an eating disorder.

Maybe we should all just bite the bullet and explain to Mrs. Carmichael what was really going on. This was getting too serious. If Angelina was anorexic, her mom was going to have to know about it. I would just have to convince Angelina of that.

That's me. Always on the lookout for easy things to do with my day.

On the way to Angelina's, I passed a newsstand. Pictures of shiny-haired women stared at me from the racks. I thought about all the girls I'd seen in the rest room and at the mall making faces at their own reflections, as if they were dissatisfied with what they were seeing. Were pictures like these the problem?

At the bus stop, a big photo showed skinny-mini model Kate Moss holding up a bottle of perfume. I remembered the statistics. Kate Moss represented less than 4% of American women. Yet it was her image so many girls felt they had to live up to. Wanted to imitate.

I had a feeling that this didn't include her bouts in the hospital. Did anyone talk about that?

Someone had left a magazine behind on the bench at the bus stop. I picked it up and flipped through it. Now that Toni had pointed out all those photography techniques, it was a lot easier to see how fake these pictures really were.

I tossed the magazine into the garbage can where it belonged. All those articles were about how to look a certain way, dress a certain way and weigh a certain weight. Didn't they know we have more on our minds?

I arrived at Angelina's, wondering how I could get her to talk to her mom.

"Hi, Casey," Angelina said. She looked puzzled.

"I need to talk to you," I explained.

"Come on in."

As I stepped inside I could hear Mrs. Carmichael ordering someone around in the next room. It sounded like she didn't get the right items from some catalogue or something.

Angelina lowered her voice. "Did you figure out who's doing this to me?"

"Angelina, you're going to be off the squad if your weight drops too low," I blurted.

Angelina looked kind of stunned. "I . . . I don't weigh too little," she stammered.

"You hardly eat and you're really small," I argued. "The coach told me there are minimum weight requirements—"

"Casey." Angelina cut me off. "I just take after my mom. We have small bones."

Mrs. Carmichael entered. "Hello, and you are?"

Was she afraid I was going to contaminate her precious Angelina with my non-pep? "I'm here to try to stop the person who has been bugging Angelina."

"Oh? That's very nice of you. Would you like a diet soda?"

Gross. "No thanks."

Lauren stalked into the room and plopped down on the couch. She swung her feet toward the coffee table.

"Feet off the table," Mrs. Carmichael ordered without even looking.

I decided to tell Mrs. Carmichael about all the pranks, since I had a feeling Angelina wouldn't.

It was time to get things out in the open. I didn't think the perp was ready to quit. "Mrs. Carmichael . . ." I launched in and didn't pause until I'd spilled everything. I was afraid that if I gave her a chance, she'd jump in and downplay everything. But to my surprise, she listened.

"We have to go to the principal," Mrs. Carmichael said after she heard the whole story.

"No!" Angelina shouted. "If we do that it will only make things worse. The person will get really really mad, and then who knows what they'll do?"

"Hide a pom-pom," Lauren muttered.

"Lauren!" Mrs. Carmichael snarled.

"I know what I *should* do," Angelina declared. "I should quit the squad. Just until Casey figures out who's behind all this. Casey's really smart. She'll solve it."

"No!" Mrs. Carmichael did her barking thing again. "No, no, no! That is only giving them what they want. And I refuse to do that!"

I agreed with Mrs. Carmichael—to a point. On the other hand, I couldn't see how Angelina would do well in a competition when she was this spooked.

"End of discussion," Mrs. Carmichael announced. "You will stay on the squad. It's simply too important to you."

I was beginning to wonder who thought it was more important—Angelina or her mom.

Mrs. Carmichael plastered a big smile on her face. Obviously she was finished with this conversation. "Angelina, why don't you show your friend our cheerleader corner?"

Was that where cheerleaders got sent when they misbehaved?

"Kill yourself now," Lauren warned.

"Lauren, I am losing patience with you."

I followed Mrs. Carmichael through the hallway to the study. It was filled with clippings, trophies and photos of Mrs. Carmichael as a cheerleader. There was almost as much stuff here as there was in Coach Seltzer's office.

Only in Coach Seltzer's office there were pictures of lots of different girls. Here there were two faces and two faces only— Mrs. Carmichael's and Angelina's.

In fact, I didn't see any pictures of Lauren anywhere in the house. Maybe she was in the baby pictures. But after a certain age, she vanished. She was the invisible daughter.

Ouch. That must hurt.

"Do you . . . do you want to see our room?" Angelina asked.

"Sure." All those cheerleader pictures made me itchy.

Angelina's room had a split personality. One side was such a pigsty it made my room look like it had maid service. The other side was so neat it was hard to imagine someone even lived in it.

Angelina sat on the neatly made bed. I had figured that was her side.

If I'd looked a moment longer, I would have known for sure. Beside the bed was a bookcase full of books about dinosaurs. A huge collection of dinosaur models was on a shelf. These weren't those cutsey stuffed dinos, either. These were detailed replicas. Some of them were skeletons put together bone by bone.

"You're really into this dinosaur stuff."

"I'm trying to figure out the best way to group my collection," Angelina said. "I think one day I'd like to work in a museum. You know, make exhibits and things."

She showed me the models and told me different dinosaur facts. It dawned at me that she probably liked dinosaurs so much because they were her opposite. She said she liked them because they were big and powerful. Angelina was small, and with this mysterious person after her—and her mother—she must feel pretty powerless.

"Once I get a family group finished I'm going to make little cards like for a real exhibit," she continued. "I'd ask Lauren to help me, because she's really artistic, but she sort of hates me."

As if on cue, Lauren stomped into the room. "Oh, great," she grumbled. "Now I have to put up with your friends, too."

Angelina looked crushed. I could tell she wished she could be friends with her sister.

Lauren got down on her stomach and reached under the bed. Out came a jar of peanut butter and a chocolate bar. "Don't say a word," she warned us. She grabbed her Walkman, went into the bathroom and slammed the door.

This was an uncomfortable moment. To avoid looking at Angelina I got up and checked out the room. A big potted plant stood by the window. I went over to look at it.

I found more than I bargained for. Behind the curtain, I saw some dried-out carrots. In the dirt of the plant, I found a half-buried sandwich.

It looked like Angelina was hiding food that she was supposed to be eating. So Lauren was bingeing in the bathroom, while Angelina starved herself. This was one pressure-cooker household.

Before I could turn around, Mrs. Carmichael came in, carrying a zippered garment bag.

"Here's your uniform. Just back from the dry cleaners," Mrs. Carmichael gushed. "Raring to go."

The bathroom door opened, and Lauren

glared out at us. "I will be soooooooo happy when cheerleading season is over!" She stormed out of the room.

My news radar beeped: Motive—*beep*. Means—*beep*. Opportunity—*beep*.

I had another suspect.

Lauren. *Beep beep beep.*

# CHAPTER 20

# Locker Room Invaded by Mad Scissorhands!

THE NEXT DAY I had a plan. I was going to rule out my other suspects before focusing on Lauren. The *Real News* deadline was Thursday. Today was Tuesday. I didn't have much time.

Neither did Angelina.

I phoned Melody and asked her to walk with me to school. We met at our usual midway point.

"I have something for you," I said. I rummaged in my backpack and pulled out the copper bracelet Megan had given me. "You left it at the sleepover."

Melody slipped it onto her wrist. "Thanks. Now if I could just find the other one."

"I think I saw it," I told her. "There was one just like this on the floor of the girls' locker room."

153

"Really? I hope it made it into the lost and found."

"I found it the day there was a bloody Barbie doll in Angelina's locker." I studied Melody's face to see if she would have a reaction.

"Ringo told me about that." Melody made a face. "Angelina, damsel in distress. I'm sick of it." She kicked a stone.

I figured that was my cue to back off. Besides, I had a new suspect to question. For some reason, Rashidah was sitting on the front steps of Trumbull.

Why was she here again? To pull something on Angelina? Time to get some answers.

"Hi, Rashidah," I greeted her. "This is my friend Melody."

"Hello."

I plopped down beside Rashidah. "Do you have the day off from Perkins Day?"

"It's some kind of teachers' conference day or something," Rashidah explained. "So I got a day pass to hang with Gary."

"Gary from *Real News*?" Melody asked.

"He's Rashidah's cousin," I explained.

"I like your braids," Melody said.

"Thanks. Your bracelet's cool."

"I made it."

They could bond later. "Rashidah is a cheerleader at Perkins Day," I told Melody.

Melody looked surprised. "Really?"

Rashidah bristled. "What, you don't think I could be?"

"No, it's not that. It's just that the cheerleaders here are all so . . . so . . ."

"Perky," I finished for Melody. I had a feeling she meant skinny, which Rashidah was not. But Melody realized where she was heading and didn't want to say it.

"Exactly," Melody said. She tossed me a grateful look. "They are so alike they're hard to tell apart."

"I know, I've seen them." Rashidah laughed.

"There seems to be a lot of pressure on how the cheerleaders look," I added.

"You don't think I look good?" Rashidah demanded.

I checked her out. She did look good. Healthy, proud, confident. She had a great hairstyle, cool clothes. Her body was bigger and curvier than the bodies of the cheerleaders on our squad. But did that mean she didn't look good? Only according to some weird standards.

"You look awesome," I told her truthfully.

"It's all about style," Rashidah said, flipping her braids. "And I know I'm stylin'."

"You've got that right," Melody agreed.

"You've got your own style, too," Rashidah told Melody.

"Has being a cheerleader helped your confidence?" I asked. "Or do you think it makes it harder because of all the pressure to look a certain way?"

"You ask a lot of questions," Rashidah commented. "Every time I see you. Are you writing a book?"

I figured it would be best if I told her at least part of the truth. "I'm writing a story for the newspaper about cheerleaders. You know, some of the nasty pranks they play on each other because of competition."

"That's just stupid kid stuff," Rashidah commented. "Total waste of time. There are more important things to worry about."

"What about the pressures to be thin?" I asked.

"Do I look like I care about that?" she demanded.

"Some girls starve themselves or make themselves throw up to maintain a certain weight," I pointed out.

Rashidah snorted. "Those skinny little white girls are all bones. Do they really think they look good like that?"

"I guess. . . ."

Rashidah stood up. "I have to hit the girls' room. Call me when you have a *real* problem." She shook her head again. "Like that stuff even matters. It works my last nerve."

She stomped away.

"Do you think she's right?" Melody asked hopefully.

"She made sense to me," I said. "But there's something bugging her. I wonder what it is."

I'd have to ask Gary. I wondered if whatever was bothering Rashidah could make her take it out on Angelina.

I walked Melody to her homeroom, and then went on to mine. I wished I could have gotten some comments from Rashidah about boys and height. It would have given me some good stuff to send to Griffin. She had attitude, but her head was on straight. She reminded me of Toni.

I had study period right after homeroom today, so I headed straight for the *Real News* office. I never got there.

"Come quick," Ringo said. "Angelina is totally freaking out in the girls' locker room."

"What happened?" I asked.

"I don't know," he said as he hurried me along. "It's the girls' locker room. I'm not allowed in, remember?"

"Then how do you know she's freaking?"

"I heard her scream, and then it sounded like she was throwing things around."

"Is anyone else in there?"

"I don't *know*," he snapped.

I cringed. "Girls' locker room, right. Sorry."

We got to the hallway that led to the entrance. Whoa. Who was that I saw? Miss Thing herself, Rashidah. She stood talking to Gary just in front of the locker room door. Gary glanced over, and what did he do? He pulled Rashidah down the hallway the other way.

Suspicious or what?

"Wait here," I told Ringo. "I promise to come back out with information."

I braced myself for anything. "Angelina?" I called.

No answer.

I cleared my throat and tried again. "Angelina?" I called louder. I came around to the row where Angelina's locker was.

She sat on the floor. Things were scattered across the tiles. It looked like everything from her locker had been tossed onto the floor.

"They got into your locker again?" I asked.

Angelina nodded.

"Did they empty your stuff onto the floor?"

Angelina looked embarrassed. "I did that," she confessed. "I was upset."

"What upset you?" What upset me was not being able to figure out how the perp kept getting into Angelina's locked locker. It was driving me loco!

Silently she handed me a pile of red-and-white fabric.

Her uniform had been slashed to pieces.

"Wow," I murmured. "They must hate you." I caught a glimpse of Angelina's pale face. "Sorry, it just popped out."

"I know." Angelina sighed. "I can't take this anymore. I'm all jittery all the time. I'm having bad dreams." She buried her face in her hands. "And I'm supposed to ignore this? How can I? I can't perform in the meet . . . I just can't."

What could I say? Between the incidents and the non-eating, she seemed a candidate for serious disaster. "I'm doing everything I can to figure out who the person is," I told her.

"I know you are." Angelina sighed. "But I think that might be why the person did this."

"I don't follow."

"They know you're investigating so they got even madder. I think you should drop the whole thing."

I gaped at her. "No way!"

I wasn't going to back off the story now. Besides, I thought her theory was wrong. "I think the pranks are escalating because you're getting closer to the competition."

"What will I do about my uniform?" she wailed.

"You'll have to tell Coach Seltzer," I said. "She'll get you a new one."

"I'm afraid she might punish the squad over this. And I'm *sure* no one on the team would do this to me."

"You see," I pointed out. "That's why you need me to keep investigating. To prove that it wasn't one of your teammates."

"I guess," she said reluctantly. "All I know is, I can't take much more."

"I know."

We left the locker room and I told Ringo about the uniform. He walked her to her next class. She was going to be late. I had a feeling a tardy notice was nothing compared to having your uniform slashed.

One good thing came out of this latest episode. It cleared Melody.

That uniform had been at Angelina's house last night. I had seen it. So whoever slashed it had to do it right after Angelina stashed it in her locker—during homeroom.

Melody was with me the entire time.

Rashidah, on the other hand, had no homeroom to be in. And I'd seen her at the scene of the crime.

I needed to have a serious talk with Gary. Could he be helping Rashidah? Maybe covering for her unknowingly?

Nah. I could see Gary helping Rashidah spy— maybe telling her when the cheerleading practices were. But he wouldn't do anything to hurt Angelina. That just wasn't his style.

Rashidah's style was more aggressive. Aggressive enough to do this?

Big old maybe.

# Karma Rebounds and Bounces Through Cafeteria!

WHEN IT WAS time for lunch, I sat with the rah-rahs. I think we were getting used to each other. Or maybe I was getting better at filtering out their chatter. I just didn't hear all the squealing and gushing and pepping anymore.

"That is so scary," Samantha said after Angelina filled them in on the latest.

"Whoever is doing this," Ringo assured her, "will face serious karma rebound."

Angelina looked worried. "Do you think?"

"What is karma rebound?" Tara asked.

"What goes around, comes around," Ringo explained. "This negative vibe action will boomerang back to the baddie."

"Don't worry," Marcy said. "From now on, you

won't go to your locker by yourself. One of us will always be there."

"Thanks," Angelina said. She gazed down at her sandwich. "It's nice to know you're all on my side."

"Of course we are," Samantha gushed. "We need you to be at your best at the cheerleading meet. You're our lead stunt girl."

"Time is running out," Marcy agreed. "I was so surprised when Coach Seltzer called off practice yesterday. Especially since Angelina has already missed so many."

"We'll help you catch up," Tara promised. "We'll drill and drill and drill until you are so perfect we're a shoo-in."

Angelina bit her lip. She studied her sandwich, then held it out to Ringo. "I'm not very hungry. Do you want it? It's hummus."

Tara's nose crinkled. "Eww."

"I'll try anything," Ringo said gamely. "What's hummus?"

"Mashed-up chickpeas," Angelina explained. "A lot of vegetarians eat it."

Ringo took a big bite. "Tasty," he said. He thought for a minute as he chewed. "Awesome. Chickpeas are kinda sorta like peanut butter."

"It's kind of the same texture," Angelina conceded. "But they taste different to me."

Peanut butter? Wasn't Angelina severely allergic to it?

I snatched the sandwich from Ringo and sniffed it.

"No need to get grabby," Ringo said. "If you wanted a taste all you had to do was ask."

I took a bite. "This is definitely peanut butter."

I eat the stuff almost every day. I know peanut butter.

"Aren't you allergic to peanut butter?" Samantha asked. "Why would your mom give it to you for lunch?"

I shook my head in disbelief. Samantha's escalator obviously didn't get to the top floor. "Angelina's mom didn't give her this sandwich," I explained. "The perp did."

The whole table gasped. I felt a little like Miss Marple or Nancy Drew when they reveal the secret identity of the murderer.

Only I wasn't quite ready to do that. Almost. But not quite.

But this had become dangerous. Didn't Angelina tell us she almost died when she ate peanut butter? Who would go that far? Who had so much at stake?

I was pretty sure I knew, but I still had some questions.

Angelina stood up and grabbed her backpack.

"Where are you going?" Ringo asked.

"To Coach Seltzer. I'm quitting the team."

"You can't!" Marcy burst out.

"I can, and I will."

I grabbed Angelina's skinny wrist. "Hold off," I told her. "I am almost ready to name the culprit. Once I do, these pranks will stop."

A terrified look crossed Angelina's face. "I can't live like this. I don't care who it is!" She yanked her wrist out of my grip. For an elf, she could be pretty strong. And strong-minded.

"I'll go with you," Ringo offered.

Angelina was so obviously upset that the Frosted Cheerios didn't even tease her about Ringo. I figured I'd get the lowdown on the meeting with the coach from Ringo later. Right now I needed to find Gary and Rashidah. They weren't in the cafeteria.

I didn't think Rashidah would know anything about Angelina's peanut butter allergy. It's not one of those public knowledge kind of things. But I had to make sure.

I found Gary exactly where I thought I would. In the gym. I guess he liked to soak up the sweaty atmosphere.

Rashidah was on the far side of the gym. She had gotten into a soccer game. Good. That meant I could question Gary openly.

"I see your cousin has found some pals," I said as I sat beside him.

He slid into a more vertical position. "Yeah. She finds ways to fit in."

Enough chitchat. "Okay, Gary. Why has she been hanging around here so much? It's not because Trumbull serves better food than Perkins Day, because that's impossible."

"Why does it matter?" he asked.

"Gary, hello? She's from one of the rival cheerleading teams? The best cheerleader on our squad is being tormented into dropping out. Any of this ring a bell to you?"

"It's not like that."

"Then tell me what it is like."

Gary rubbed his face and watched Rashidah. "Rashidah's parents are going through a wicked bad divorce. So Rashidah is staying with us during this custody thing."

"Why has she been here, instead of at her own practice?"

"Don't spread this around, okay? Rashidah and her parents have family counseling every week, and it interferes with her practice. She had to quit the squad."

"I know she's spying," I told Gary.

"So? There's no crime in watching the other team. She's still big with her girls. She wants to help any way she can."

"Big enough to take out Angelina?"

"No way."

"When did you first see Rashidah today?" I asked. I wondered if she had the time to get to Angelina's locker after I had seen her on the steps.

"Just after you did. I was inside. I spotted you guys talking on the steps. She was with me all morning."

Well, Gary confirmed what I had suspected. Rashidah might have motive, but she didn't do the crime.

Besides, I was pretty sure these latest incidents were put into motion at Angelina's house. The uniform had probably been slashed and repacked into that shiny suit bag Mrs. Carmichael kept it in. The sandwich was slipped into Angelina's dinosaur lunchbox.

Angelina's big sister, Lauren, was the perp.

# CHAPTER 22

# Reporter Uncovers Sinister Sister Act!

I KNEW WHAT I had to do and that I had to do it fast. As soon as school ended I would go to Angelina's house and confront Lauren myself.

What a front-page story this would make! Complete with a confession!

The minute the bell rang I raced out of school. I ran into Ringo. He looked bummed.

"Did Angelina quit the squad?" I asked.

He nodded. "Coach Seltzer didn't even try to talk her out of it."

I had a feeling I knew why. It saved the coach the trouble of asking Angelina to leave because of her eating disorder.

"I wonder what Mrs. Carmichael is going to say," I mused. "She's got cheer fever."

"Angelina begged Coach Seltzer to break the

news to her mom," Ringo told me. "I think she's more afraid of her mom than of the perp."

I could believe that. I almost felt sorry for Lauren. Once Mrs. Carmichael found out what was going on, well, I just knew I didn't want to even be in the neighborhood for that fight.

I couldn't worry about Lauren, though. I had a story to get and a perp to stop. Then Angelina could go back to cheerleading with enough time to get in shape for the meet.

Mrs. Carmichael answered the door. "I'm sorry, Casey. Angelina isn't here. She's at cheerleading practice."

Hm. I guess the news that Angelina quit hadn't hit yet. Well, maybe it wouldn't have to. "Actually, I'm here to talk to Lauren."

Mrs. Carmichael looked surprised. Then she shrugged. "Lauren's upstairs in her room. As usual."

I trudged up the stairs. I ran over all the facts so that I wouldn't blow it. Lauren was a tough girl. I needed to be prepared.

I knocked.

"Go away," Lauren shouted from inside the room.

This was not starting out well.

I opened the door and poked in my head. "It's me."

Lauren was sprawled on her bed. "Angelina's not here."

I stepped into the room. "I know. I wanted to talk to you."

"Why?" She gazed at me suspiciously.

"You really hate all this cheerleader stuff, don't you?" I said. "Me, too. It's so bogus."

I thought if she believed we had something in common I'd get her to slip up.

"Little kids bugging me is bogus," she said.

Okay, so I was wrong about getting her to reveal anything. I'd just have to go after her with what I knew.

"Okay, Lauren. Let's just cut to the chase. Fact: You hate cheerleaders. Fact: Your mom throws Angelina in your face every chance she gets. Fact: You've had plenty of opportunities to pull off the pranks that have been tormenting Angelina."

I paused for a breath. I was surprised she let me keep speaking. I figured she wasn't used to anyone talking this way to her—especially a "little kid" like me.

She sneered. "I don't know where you're heading with this list of so-called facts. Quit bothering me."

"You quit bothering Angelina."

Now she just stared at me.

Just then Angelina stepped into the room. She looked back and forth between us. "Wh-what's going on?" she stammered.

I put my hands on my hips. "I'm waiting for Lauren to confess that she's the perp," I declared.

"What?" Lauren and Angelina said in unison.

"Think about it, Angelina," I said. "She has opportunity. She has all-important access. These last two pranks could only have been accomplished here at your house." I explained how the uniform must have been repacked in the garment bag and that the sandwich had been switched at home.

"But . . . but . . ." Angelina sputtered.

"You are so off base," Lauren said. "Get out of my room!"

"It's Angelina's room, too!" I retorted. I dropped down and pulled the jar of peanut butter out from under Lauren's bed. I showed it to Angelina. "I'd be willing to bet this was what your sandwich was made with."

"Back off, squirt," Lauren snarled.

Griffin was right. It didn't feel good to be called a squirt.

"No. I'm going to tell your mom what's been going on right now. And then I'm writing it all up as a front-page story for *Real News*."

"You can't do that!" Angelina burst out. She

sank to the floor. Tears began streaming down her face.

"I know it's upsetting to think that your own sister could go after you like this, but—"

"Lauren didn't do it!" she cut me off. "I did!"

# CHAPTER 23

# Boy Caught in Friendship Triangle!

I STARED AT Angelina. So did Lauren.

"You pulled all those pranks on yourself?" This made no sense to me.

Angelina wiped her face with her fingers and nodded. "I couldn't think of any other way my mom would let me quit the team."

"You did all this because you *don't* want to be a cheerleader?" Talk about extreme. But after seeing Mrs. Carmichael in action I could understand that normal measures might not work.

"You have to tell your mom," I said.

"Tell me what?"

All heads whipped toward the doorway. Angelina had left the door open, and now Mrs. Carmichael loomed in it.

"Angelina, what are you doing home so early?"

She spotted Angelina's tear-stained face. "Lauren, what have you done now?" she demanded.

"Of course, you think this is my fault," Lauren snapped. "Hah! It's *yours*!"

Mrs. Carmichael stepped into the room. "What on earth do you mean?"

Angelina stayed mute. I took charge. Someone had to. I laid it all out—how Angelina had been doing all these things to herself so she'd have an excuse to drop out of the squad.

"I don't understand," Mrs. Carmichael said. "You love cheerleading. Why would you want to quit?"

Was the woman deaf? "She *doesn't* love cheerleading," I said. I really wished Angelina would say something. Mrs. Carmichael looked at me as if I was making everything up.

Then she smiled as if she had figured it all out. "You're just feeling the stress of your first competition, sweetie."

She knelt down and gave Angelina a quick hug. "It happens to all of us on the pep squad." She smoothed Angelina's hair. "I promise you won't feel so nervous after this first meet."

I realized something scary. Angelina could starve herself off the team now that Plan A hadn't worked.

Mrs. Carmichael stood up and straightened

her skirt. "Now wash your face, and we'll have no more silly talk of quitting. What's our saying? When the going gets tough . . ."

"The tough get going," Angelina murmured. She sounded like a robot.

I couldn't take it. "Don't you get it? She doesn't want to be a cheerleader, okay?"

Mrs. Carmichael's jaw set. "Casey, it's time for you to go. We've taken care of things here."

"If Angelina doesn't quit she might die!" I blurted.

That got their attention. "You already said there is no culprit," Mrs. Carmichael said evenly.

I plunged ahead. "Coach Seltzer told me that she might have to ask one or two of the girls to leave the team because their weight was getting dangerously low."

"Angelina is just small boned. And she watches her weight, like I do." Mrs. Carmichael said that as if it was a point of pride.

"It's more than that," I insisted. "Angelina shows all the signs of an eating disorder. A really danger-ous one called anorexia." I turned to Angelina. She looked stricken. "I'm sorry, but I think it's true."

"I think it is, too," Lauren said. She got up from her bed and sat beside Angelina on the floor. "I've seen you hide food."

"Angelina?" Mrs. Carmichael said.

"It's true," Angelina whispered.

Mrs. Carmichael sighed. "Well, well, well. All right then, if it matters that much to you, you can quit cheerleading. For now."

Amazing. She didn't even acknowledge the big galumphing problem staring her in the face: Angelina's eating disorder.

"Casey, run along. We have some things to talk about here." Mrs. Carmichael crossed her arms. "In private."

"Okay. Angelina, I'll see you tomorrow."

She didn't look at me, but she nodded.

I let myself out. I felt flattened. There wasn't anything more I could do.

I didn't have a good feeling about Angelina. Her mom just didn't want to see the problem. The only hopeful sign was that Lauren seemed almost sympathetic. Maybe now she wouldn't treat Angelina so much like the enemy.

At least the first step was taken. The problem was out in the open.

How out in the open should it be? And could I write the story now that the culprit was Angelina? *What* story?

The next day I went to talk to Megan. As much as I hated to admit it, when it came to decisions like this, she had good judgment.

I laid it all out. I just couldn't decide if it was news or not. No one in the school, other than the team, had known about the incidents. It's not as if the entire student body had to know. The only person truly affected was Angelina herself. And Ringo, of course. Now that Angelina was off the team, he'd be participating in the meet.

But I couldn't let go of the story. I knew it was an important one. Only if I printed it, everyone would know about Angelina's emotional problems—and that didn't seem like a way to help her get better. It would only give kids ammunition.

"You've got to write about the issue," Megan agreed. "It's so important. But it won't be a front-page story."

"I know." It killed me to see that front-page spot taken by somebody else. Maybe I should have gone with the retiring teacher story after all.

But I knew that the investigation had uncovered important facts. And maybe some of those facts would get Angelina to get the help she needed.

"So just a straight sports story?" Gary asked

after I told him Megan's decision. "My offer still stands. You can cover the meet."

"Uh, no thanks, Gary," I said, grinning. At least I hadn't lost my sense of humor. "I know how much it means to you. I'd hate to take it away from you."

While I was online at the *Real News* office, I sent Griffin a quick note. I told him Angelina's whole sad story. Then I reminded him that some of the most famous hunks, like Tom Cruise and Mel Gibson, are short.

**To: Wordpainter**
**From: Thebeast**
Thanks for the heightness update. Guess what? I made the soccer team! And I'm not even the smallest guy on it. And height's not a factor in soccer. You don't need to be tall to be good.

Did you know that soccer is one of the world's most popular sports?

I grinned. He seemed to be back to his old self. Phew.

Ringo shuffled in carrying his sketch pad. "Megan, I have a Simon for the body-image theme." He held it out for us to see.

Beauty IS in the Eye of the Beholder.

"Excellent!" Megan said.

"Another skewed Ringo view," I added. "I like it."

Gary thumped him on the back. "So I hear you're in the meet after all."

Ringo shrugged. "Yeah. I feel kind of bad that Angelina had to drop out so I could be there."

"Angelina had been trying to drop out for a long time," I assured him. "You're not taking away something she wants. She will be much happier this way, believe me."

He studied me for a moment. "Okay, I believe you." He did some shoulder rolls. "I have a lot of practicing to get in. The meet is on Saturday. Uh, Coach Casey . . . ?" He knelt and posed like a begging puppy.

"Okay, okay, stop going all pathetic." I laughed. "I'll be there."

I typed up my story. It felt good to get it down on paper.

```
        The Secret Monster:
        Body-Image Disorders
          By Casey Smith


    There is an invisible enemy
among us. It can strike at the
strangest times. It makes kids
starve. It forces kids to throw
up. It pressures kids to hate
themselves.
    This enemy has many weapons at
its disposal. Magazines, television,
gossip, films, posters, makeover
specialists, the weight-loss
industry, drug companies. All
these forces help this enemy to
get what it wants.
    What it wants is your self-
esteem. Your sense of self. Your
ideas about who you are and what
```

you can be. This force is powerful.
And it is using us.

Good opening, I told myself.

One of the things I had read was that anorexia is a disease of control. I could see that with Angelina. She felt like all she had control over was what food went into her mouth. On top of that, her mom rewarded thinness and dieting.

As I worked on the editorial, I realized that writing was my access to control. Writing helped me feel less powerless. I took in the world around me, processed it and then sent it back out. On good days, I even made a difference. And it had nothing to do with my looks.

I handed Megan my piece and dropped by the field. To my surprise, Melody and Angelina were both there, coaching Ringo.

"Bring your left hand higher while you move your right leg," Melody instructed Ringo.

He made a move.

"No, your *right* leg," Melody corrected.

"Wait!" Angelina charged over to Ringo and drew a picture on his right hand.

He grinned. "Raptor means right," he declared, displaying the little ink drawing on his right hand. "Right."

Melody looked peeved. "Okay, Ringo. Let's try

this again," she ordered. "Kick and turn."

"Twist and up!" Angelina shouted. "Twist and up!"

Ringo tried to follow both sets of orders. Only somehow his body wasn't going along with it. He twisted and leaped, a flying pretzel.

I shook my head. This Angelina, Melody and Ringo triangle was obviously still part of the Trumbull geometry.

Did I really think everything would be solved once I nailed my story?

Get real!

# My Word
## *by Linda Ellerbee*

MY NAME IS LINDA ELLERBEE. This book is especially close to my heart. Society telling us how we're supposed to look isn't new; it happened when I was your age. But the emphasis on being thin enough or tall enough or pretty enough has only gotten worse in the last few years.

The number of teens with eating disorders is at an all-time high. And it's certainly not just girls with issues about how they look. I have spoken with parents who've chosen to give their sons experimental drugs in order to make the boys grow taller. What, you ask, is going on here?

Basically, it's a plot. No, really, it is. In order to sell magazines, clothes, shoes, makeup, nail polish, perfume, exercise equipment and even underwear, we need to be made to think that these things will make us better, somehow. If you're already satisfied with yourself, you might not want to buy what someone wants to sell you.

But here's the deal. We who care about you want very much for you to believe you are okay just the way you are, and that you don't have to look anorexic to be beautiful. However, obesity in teenagers is also at an all-time high, so we also want to send a message that teenagers should eat right and exercise because carrying too much weight causes health problems. If they sound like conflicting messages, well, they are—and that's a problem.

The other problem is that, as usual, we grown-ups can really underestimate how smart you are. Once on *Nick News* we produced a special about body image. A girl told me that her mother didn't want her playing with Barbie dolls. Stupidly, I began to lecture her. I told her that perhaps her mom was worried because most of us are never going to look like Barbie; we aren't that thin, our waists aren't that tiny and we don't run around on tippy-toes all the time. I said that maybe her mom was concerned that if her daughter thought Barbie was how women were supposed to look, she'd think bad of herself if she didn't grow up and look that way. I went on . . . and on . . . and on . . .

Finally, the girl, who was eleven, interrupted me. "Uh . . . Linda?"

"Yes?" I said, slowing down in my rant, but only slightly.

"Linda, it's a doll."

Thank you. I needed to remember that. I

needed to remember that kids (you!) are smarter than we think, that you can separate the real from the unreal and that you and your generation can be (must be) the group that puts an end to the notion that there's only one standard of beauty.

Can you do that? Can you change the world?

Get real.

# Girl Reporter Bytes Back!

"YOU THINK YOU'RE so smart," Toni yelled. She gestured at me with the Alienhead. "You always have to . . ." She stopped yelling and glanced at the critter. Her dark brows knit together.

She studied the Alienhead. I wasn't sure what was going on, but I was glad that she had stopped blasting me. She just kept squeezing the Alienhead's feet. Her expression went from puzzled to frantic.

"Is something wrong?" Megan asked.

Toni picked up each of the Alienheads figurines, inspecting them closely. She squeezed their feet, tapped their heads, did everything except pull out a stethoscope to check if they were breathing.

"Toni, are your Alienheads sick or something?" Ringo asked.

"Worse." She held up the biggest figurine. "They're fake!"